How To Successfully Reclaim Your Family

1. Arrive at your beloved's cozy inn under an assumed name—and with a new face.

2. Form an instant attachment to her adorable toddler, who bears a striking resemblance to the man you used to be.

3. Touch her wary heart with your gruff tenderness.

4. Reveal your true identity and then fight tooth and nail to make up for lost time with your family.

5. Soften your lady love's resolve with electrifying gazes, soul-searing kisses—and sweet promises of more to come....

FAMILY

Elizabeth AUGUST

Joey's Father

MARRIED FOR A MINUTE

Silhouette Books

Published by Silhouette Books

America's Publisher of Contemporary Romance

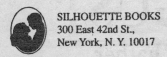

SILHOUETTE BOOKS
300 East 42nd St.,
New York, N. Y. 10017

ISBN 0-373-82166-2

JOEY'S FATHER

Copyright © 1990 by Elizabeth August

This edition published by arrangement with Harlequin Books S.A.

® and TM are trademarks of Harlequin Books S.A., used under license. Trademarks indicated with ® are registered in the United States Patent and Trademark Office, the Canadian Trade Marks Office and in other countries.

Visit us at www.romance.net

Printed in U.S.A.

Dear Reader,

One of the themes in this book—that real love is not dampened because external appearances change—became very real to me the winter of 1997-98. I was diagnosed with a large cancerous tumor in my abdomen. After the surgery to remove it, I underwent several months of chemotherapy. So there I was...a fifty-three-year-old woman with a disfiguring scar, a few straggly hairs left on my head and strain lines on my face from always feeling tired and ill.

And yet my husband constantly told me that I looked cute, and his tender attentiveness was proof that he meant what he said. We had been married for more than thirty years and, like all couples, had had our ups and downs. But we always got past the rocky moments and I thought we were as close to each other as any couple could get. I was wrong. During those trying months, we grew even closer and his love gave me the strength I needed to endure. I am so very thankful we found each other.

Dear reader, I hope you will forgive me. This is more a love letter to my husband than a letter to you. Life happens, and to know that his hand will always be held out to me to grab on to when I need help is a blessing for which I will always be grateful. For you, I hope you have found this same kind of love or will find it.

Elizabeth August

Please address questions and book requests to:
Silhouette Reader Service
U.S.: 3010 Walden Ave., P.O. Box 1325, Buffalo, NY 14269
Canadian: P.O. Box 609, Fort Erie, Ont. L2A 5X3

To Joyce, for all of her support and
for being a terrific agent.

Chapter One

"**S**o you saw her?" Brant Mallery paused to gaze unseeingly out the window at the Boston skyline as a woman's face filled his mind. Brown eyes darkened by passion to near ebony stared back at him. Soft warm lips, gently swollen from a long kiss, invited another. The nose was straight, medium in size. A sudden longing filled him as he recalled the cute way she had of crinkling it when she was teasing. Although to others that face was merely pleasant, to him it had been beautiful. But that was a long time ago. A great many things had changed for him and, no doubt, for the woman, as well. A determined coolness spread through him, erasing all trace of the rekindled longing.

Paul Johnson shifted uneasily in the plush leather chair. Giving himself time to think, he let his gaze travel around the interior of Brant Mallery's mahogany-paneled office. In the far corner near a wide window was the comfortable chair grouping, used when Brant wanted a casual atmosphere for business. In front of him was the oversize mahogany desk Brant sat behind when he felt intimidation was necessary to get what he wanted. Admitting that he'd already mentally practiced every possible way of saying what he had to say, Paul again studied the younger man standing rigidly by the window. He had known Brant since Brant's birth thirty years ago. Through the years, Brant had become as astute a businessman as his father had been. He was also as tough. He had to have been to have survived that accident nearly three years ago. The problem was, Paul wasn't certain how Brant was going to take this news. He cleared his throat. "There's something you should know."

Brant turned to face the other occupant of the room. Paul Johnson was in his sixties, a tall lean man with thinning white hair and a distinguished carriage. He had been Brant's lawyer and his father's lawyer before him. He was a close, trusted friend, and Brant knew that particular clearing of the throat. It always preceded an unsettling disclosure. "What should I know?" he demanded.

"Maybe you should sit down," Paul suggested.

"Out with it!" Brant growled. Two weeks ago when he'd asked Paul to make a slight detour on his vacation and stop by Oak Valley, Maine, to covertly check on Jessie, he'd told himself he was only asking out of a sense of duty. After all, she had been his wife once, even if it had been only a four-day marriage. But during the two weeks he'd had to wait for information, his patience had grown thin. That was the problem where Jessie was concerned, he mused dryly—he'd never had any patience.

Paul decided there was no way to say this but bluntly. "She has a son. He's going to turn two in a couple of weeks."

Brant stared at the lawyer. Jessie had a son who was nearly two? Mentally he ticked off the months. A pregnancy would explain the question that had nagged at him these past years. When he'd regained consciousness following the accident, he'd told Paul... A bitter smile crossed his face. He hadn't "told" Paul. He hadn't been able to speak for months. He'd had to communicate everything in writing. Anyway, he'd informed Paul about his marriage to Jessie and ordered him to terminate it. He'd instructed the lawyer to draw up divorce papers that included an alimony payment that would allow Jessie to live comfortably. But she'd refused to accept anything. Under the circumstances, Paul had suggested an annulment. She'd agreed, then changed her mind and demanded a divorce instead. Now he understood; with a divorce the child wouldn't have been born a bastard. "My son," he said aloud, as if needing to hear himself say it to believe it.

Paul nodded. "He's the spitting image of you at that age. Same dark brown hair, same brown eyes."

But the father wouldn't resemble the son now, Brant thought cynically. Not after all the plastic surgery and facial reconstruction that had to be done following the accident. Again Jessie's image entered his mind. How could she have done this to him? How could she have had a son, *his* son, and not even have had the courtesy to inform him? His jaw twitched with controlled anger. "She had no right to keep this from me."

"You were the one who initiated the divorce proceedings," Paul reminded him. He knew Brant had been trying to be fair when he had divorced Jessica Brody, but she hadn't known that.

"That didn't give her the right to keep the boy a secret," Brant snapped. "A man should be told if he has a child."

Paul didn't like the cold anger he was seeing in Brant's eyes. It usually meant trouble. He thought of the young woman with the brown hair and friendly smile. He should have found a more subtle way of telling Brant. Again, he attempted to defend the woman. "Maybe she thought you wouldn't be interested. The two of you only knew one another for a couple of weeks and your request for a divorce came as a shock to her. It would be reasonable for her to assume you wouldn't be interested in the child."

"Maybe," Brant conceded grimly. "But I plan to correct that oversight on her part as quickly as possible." A worried look suddenly shadowed his face. "Did she recognize you?"

"No." Paul shook his head. "You were still in pretty bad shape when the divorce was being worked out. I didn't feel safe leaving you alone long enough to make the trips to Maine myself. I sent Gyles instead."

The worried look was replaced by an expression of cold calculation. "Good. I wouldn't want her bolting with the boy before I can correct this oversight on her part."

Jessica Brody Mallery, Jessie to her friends, hung up the phone and drew a tired breath. She'd just finished canceling her last reservation. Well, almost her last. There was still Mr. John Adams. His secretary had made reservations for him without leaving a phone number where he could be reached in case of a problem. The woman had explained that he was traveling and she couldn't contact him. At that time Jessie hadn't worried. It had never occurred to her

that her son, Joey, would come down with the
mumps. When he had, she had decided it was only
right that she call her preregistered guests and warn
them. She also offered to make reservations for them
at another of the local inns. When two of the first
three people she called opted for a change of accom-
modations, she decided to close the inn for the next
two weeks. It was a slow time of year anyway—she
was never heavily booked in September. Besides,
there were some repairs that needed taking care of,
and she wanted to paint the reception area and the
lounge. As for Mr. Adams, she'd called the Jeffer-
sons and they had room for him at Mountain View.
She'd send him there when he arrived.

"I can use this time to get the inn shipshape," she
reasoned aloud, refusing to worry about the loss of
revenue. She had enough in her emergency fund to
cover the closing and she was looking forward to
spending some extra time with Joey.

In spite of the fire in the fireplace, a chill suddenly
shook her as her gaze traveled around the empty
lounge area beyond the reception desk. Her jaw
tensed as she remembered the last time she had
closed the inn. It had been for her honeymoon. The
image of a dark-haired, dark-eyed man entered un-
bidden into her mind. Brant Mallery. It had been
midafternoon one day in early January when he had
first come through her door. As hard as she'd tried

to eradicate him from her memory, she could still picture him as clearly as if it had been only yesterday. He had been one of the most strikingly handsome men she'd ever seen. He'd also been one of the most tired looking.

"I'd like a room," he'd said in something close to a growl. "And then I don't want to be disturbed."

His manners, she'd thought as she registered him, could have used some improvement.

He'd insisted on carrying his own suitcase upstairs. She'd guided him to his room, and that was the last she saw of him that afternoon and evening.

It had been nearly eleven that night when she heard footsteps descending the hardwood stairs. All of her guests were back in the inn and had gone to their rooms. She was in the lounge banking the fire for the night. Glancing over her shoulder, she saw him coming toward her. When he'd registered, he'd been wearing a heavy parka-style coat, but from his carriage she'd guessed he was muscular. Now he was dressed in tailor-made slacks and a designer sweater, and she could see she had guessed right. One of the wealthy elite who works out in a gym an hour or two a day, she decided, noting that his loafers probably cost more than all her shoes put together. Her inn normally attracted a more modest clientele and she wondered why he was here. Probably got lost, she guessed. Finishing with the fire, she put the heavy night screen in front of it and turned to face him as he approached.

"I want to apologize for my grouchiness this afternoon," he said, coming to a halt near her. A thick lock of hair had fallen onto his forehead. Showing a remaining vestige of agitation, he raked it roughly back into place with his fingers. "I'd booked reservations at a resort in Massachusetts. Almost as soon as I got there I ran into people I knew. I came on this vacation to get away from everything, and the first thing I knew I was having dinner and discussing business. This morning a new group of acquaintances arrived there. I began to feel I should have stayed at home. So I checked out and started driving. I was tired and my nerves were on edge by the time I got here. To be honest, I was worried that with the luck I've been having I'd walk in and find someone I knew." He smiled crookedly. "I hope you'll accept my apology."

Jessie experienced a flutter in her stomach at the sight of his smile. "Your apology is accepted," she replied with polite reserve.

"Thanks." His smile broadened and he extended his hand toward her. "You know my name, but I don't know yours."

"It's Jessica Brody," she said, accepting his handshake. Heat like a forest fire gone wild raged through her as his large hand enfolded hers. "But everyone calls me Jessie," she added, amazed by how cool she sounded when her internal temperature felt as if it had just gone up at least ten degrees. This was crazy, she chided herself as she freed her hand and discreetly rubbed the palm against the leg of her slacks as if to erase the feel of him.

"Jessie," Brant repeated, as if testing the name. Suddenly his gaze shifted away from her and traveled around the room. When he looked at her again, his expression was shuttered. "I know it's late, but I was wondering if there was any place around here I could get something to eat."

She wondered if his sudden withdrawal was because he'd noticed her reaction to the handshake. Shrugging mentally, she decided it didn't matter. It was merely a fluke and would never happen again. "No place nearby," she replied, then added, "but I could fix you a sandwich and a piece of pie." She would have made the same offer to any of her guests under similar circumstances. What caused her a twinge of uneasiness was the realization that she actually wanted to please this particular man.

Following her into the kitchen, he leaned against a counter as she pulled out some bread and leftover roast beef. "Hope this won't get you in trouble with the boss," he said.

"I am the boss," she informed him with a casualness that belied the unsettling prickling sensation at the nape of her neck his presence was causing. "Would you like mayonnaise or mustard on your sandwich?"

"Mayonnaise," he answered.

She'd had men watch her before, but this one made her nervous, very nervous. She finished making the sandwich, cut him a piece of pie, and then put the plates on a tray. "You can have milk, water or iced tea to drink."

He chose iced tea.

Pouring him a glass, she motioned toward the door. "I hope you don't mind eating this in your room. I'm exhausted and I'd like to close up down here." She was tired, but her real problem was dealing with the unexpected effect this man was having on her. She could feel his gaze almost as if it were a physical contact, and when his fingers touched hers as he took the tray from her, a rush of heat again traveled up her arm.

I'm just overly tired, she reasoned, as she finished her chores and went up to bed.

But the next morning when she passed through the dining room on her way to the kitchen, she was acutely aware of his presence at the table by the window. She also experienced a sharp twist in her abdomen when she noticed one of her female guests giving him an inviting smile. *It's only because I don't want any trouble,* she told herself. The woman was there with her boyfriend, and Jessie didn't think he'd take very kindly to her showing an interest in another man.

Forcing herself not to think about her newest guest, Jessie was upstairs making a bed in one of the guest rooms when the prickling sensation at the nape of her neck returned. Glancing over her shoulder, she saw Brant Mallery leaning against the doorjamb watching her.

Giving the bedspread one final tuck to pull it tight, she straightened and faced him. "Is there something I can do for you, Mr. Mallery?"

"Actually I was enjoying watching you work," he replied, his gaze moving down over her loose-fitting sweater, which gave discreet evidence of the soft full mounds of her breasts, to her faded jeans, which fit her shapely hips snugly, then back up to her face.

The look of masculine approval on his face caused a pleased flush to creep up from her neck. This wasn't like her. Normally she would have greeted such male scrutiny with a cool, dismissing glance. Forcing a frown, she said, "Most of my guests prefer to enjoy the beauty of our landscape rather than watch someone clean a room."

"Normally I would, too," he conceded. Straightening away from the jamb, he continued to study her with bemused interest. "Actually I came up here to thank you for the meal last night."

"It's all part of being an innkeeper," she replied, wishing her heart wouldn't beat so erratically just because he was standing there.

"Well, thanks, anyway," he said and turned to go. Then abruptly he turned back. "I was wondering if you might have some free time later today to show me around."

She'd always made it a policy never to become involved with guests. And every instinct warned her that it would be safest to avoid this guest in particular. Although her mind formed a rejection, she heard herself saying, "If you haven't found anything better to do by two, I should be free for an hour or so then."

"Two." He confirmed their appointment with a sudden smile that caused her breath to lock in her lungs.

For the rest of the morning and into the afternoon, Jessie berated herself for breaking her own rule. Numerous times she decided she would make up some excuse to get out of their two-o'clock meeting. But when the hour rolled around, she had changed into one of her better sweater-and-slacks outfits, brushed her hair, decided it was too wayward and plaited it into a French braid down the back of her head, and even applied a light coating of makeup. "You're going to feel really silly if he's found something better to do," she'd scoffed at the image in the mirror as she gave herself one final once-over before going downstairs.

But he hadn't found anything better to do. Instead he was waiting for her at the desk.

There should be a law against any man looking that good, she had thought as she descended the stairs and he smiled up at her in greeting.

That afternoon they took a walk that lasted two hours instead of one. By the time they got back to the inn, Jessie was close to a state of panic. She had never believed in instant magnetism between a man and a woman, but she was feeling it with Brant Mallery, and its intensity frightened her. She'd seen vacation romances spring up among her guests. Nine times out of ten, they ended with one of the two people involved being badly hurt. No, vacation romances were most definitely not for her. The problem was, her body wasn't reacting to her logic.

Deciding that avoiding him would be the most prudent solution, she ate her dinner in her office and spent the evening going over papers and working on her books. Periodically she would go out into the lounge to check on the fire in the fireplace. He was always there, usually sitting alone, away from the rest of the guests, reading a book. He would look up as if he intended to speak to her, but she would quickly take care of the fire and leave. *You're hiding like a scared rabbit,* she chided herself each time she again escaped to the sanctity of her office. *I'm just being practical,* she defended.

But when she came out at eleven to bank the fire for the night, she found him waiting for her. Alone.

"If I didn't know better, I'd think you were avoiding me," he said, rising to stand behind her while she poked at the embers.

"I had a lot of work to do," she lied, finishing and sliding the screen into place.

But when she straightened and started to leave, he blocked her path. "Stay and talk with me awhile," he coaxed.

The urge to agree to anything he asked was strong. *Get out of here,* she ordered herself. "It's late and I have a full day tomorrow," she hedged, starting to circle around him.

He shifted slightly, just enough to again block her escape. "I was wondering how you ended up with a place like this," he said.

Before Jessie knew what was happening, she was sitting with him on the couch telling him about her parents, how they had bought the inn as newlyweds and how she had been born and raised here. She even told him about the accident that had cost them their lives. She didn't usually talk about that to anyone, but it seemed natural to tell Brant Mallery.

When the grandfather clock struck one she glanced

toward it in amazement. "I've got to get to bed," she said in a rush. "I have to be up at six."

"I didn't mean to keep you so long," he apologized, reaching over and combing a wayward strand of her hair off her cheek.

His touch left a trail of fire. Rising quickly, she stood waiting for him to rise and leave. But when he did stand, he remained in front of her.

"I came on this vacation because I was feeling a restlessness I couldn't dismiss," he said, gently running his fingers along the line of her jaw. "It was as though there was something missing in my life. But here with you I feel comfortable. Spend some time with me tomorrow."

The urge to agree to spend every minute with him was close to overwhelming. "I really can't," she forced herself to say. "I've always made it a policy not to socialize with my guests. I know I broke that rule today, but I think I'd better go back to it."

His finger came to rest under her chin, and gently he tilted her face up to meet his steady gaze. "You feel it, too, don't you, Jess?"

"Feel what?" she questioned. She'd wanted to sound coolly indifferent as if she didn't know what he was talking about, but instead her voice sounded shaky.

"The attraction," he elaborated. "It scares me too, Jess. But it's too strong to ignore. I spent an entire three hours, nine minutes and thirty-four seconds this evening rereading the same page over and over again, waiting for you to come out here so I could be with you.''

"The smart thing to do would be for us to stay away from each other,'' she warned.

Leaning down, he kissed her lightly. "Maybe, but I don't want to.'' He drew a terse breath. "I honestly don't think I can.'' His eyes darkened with a plea. "Spend tomorrow with me, Jess. If at the end of the day you still think the smart thing for us to do is to stay away from each other, I'll leave.''

The thought of his leaving caused her stomach to knot. "All right,'' she agreed. "I'll spend tomorrow with you.''

Later, lying in her bed, she chewed on the inside of her bottom lip. She might have agreed to the most foolish thing she would ever do in her life. But he was right about one thing—this attraction she felt to him was too strong to ignore. Spending an entire day with him might be the cure, she reasoned. It was possible this sensation he was causing within her would wear thin with increased exposure to him.

But it didn't work that way. During the next day he told her about his family, his plans for the future, what he hoped to accomplish in his life. And instead of growing away from him, she felt herself growing closer.

The next day she insisted that she could not neglect the inn another full day. But he was persistent. Every time she turned around he was there. He even came into a room she was cleaning and started to help her make a bed. She'd shooed him out. But when she'd seen him leaving the inn a few minutes later, she'd felt a sudden, tremendous void. It was accompanied by a fear, verging on panic, that he wouldn't come back.

But he came back—with an armful of roses.

On his fourth day at the inn, he proposed. "I can't imagine life without you," he said. "Marry me, Jess."

And she'd agreed. She'd never acted on impulse before, but he was someone she couldn't resist. She'd closed the inn so they could spend their honeymoon there totally alone.

Jessie blinked hard, bringing her mind back to the present. "Stupid!" she chided herself curtly. What she had thought would last a lifetime had lasted a mere four days.

A child's voice crying "Mommy" in soft, muffled tones, sounded through the portable intercom on the desk beside her. The dark shadows in her eyes faded. "At least one good thing came out of that disaster," she said with a gentle smile. When Brant Mallery had come into her life, she'd been all alone. Now she had Joey.

* * *

Brant Mallery had a stern talk with himself as he drove the rented coupe toward Oak Valley. He was going to take this slow. He wasn't going to let impatience ruin his chances for a future with his son. "She'd just better not have poisoned the boy's mind against me," he growled threateningly. But, to be fair, he admitted to himself that if she had, it was all his fault. Still, he'd done what he thought was right at the time.

Scowling grimly, he glanced at his reflection in the rearview mirror. She'd never recognize him. When he'd finally emerged from all those bandages, even his best friends hadn't known him.

He didn't like deception. But he wanted a chance to see Jessie and the boy together, size up the entire situation before they found out who he was. Even more, he wanted time to get to know his son under neutral circumstances. Once Jessie discovered his true identity, she was bound to react to him as if he were the enemy.

"All you have to do is keep your patience and temper under control, Mr. John Adams," he addressed himself sternly as he turned into the parking lot of Oak Lodge. Memories abruptly washed over him. In the moonlight, the large white frame, two-story dwelling with the wide-roofed porch looked the same as when he'd last seen it. That seemed like a lifetime ago now. In a lot of ways it was, he mused.

* * *

Jessie glanced at her watch. It was nearly 11 p.m. and Mr. Adams hadn't arrived yet. But then he'd said he might be late. He'd wired money to have her hold the room. He'd said he didn't believe in credit cards.

The frown on her face deepened. Joey was sleeping and she wanted to get some rest before he woke up again and needed attention. Rising from one of the overstuffed chairs that faced the fire, she poked at the dying embers and wondered if she should put another log on. Deciding against it, she banked the fire for the night. When Mr. Adams did arrive she wanted to just send him on his way and go directly to bed. She was about to sit down again when she heard a car.

Pulling on a coat, she went to the front door, opened it and stepped out onto the porch. A man carrying a suitcase was coming toward her. "Mr. Adams?" she asked, blocking his entrance.

"Yes," he replied. In the light of the porch lamp, she didn't look much different than she had three years ago. Her thick brunette hair hung loose around her shoulders. Her coat was unbuttoned and he noted that her style of dress hadn't changed, either. She was wearing a bulky, loose-fitting sweater and a pair of jeans. A quick appraisal also told him that she still had the kind of curves that could stir a man's blood. The only change was in her eyes; the expression in them wasn't as trusting or as open.

"I'm really sorry," Jessie explained hurriedly. "But my son has the mumps and I've decided to close down until he's no longer contagious. I've made arrangements for you to stay at the Mountain View motel. It's about thirty miles up the road. I'm sorry I couldn't find you anything closer, but we're a small community here and all the other places are fully booked. If you'll just wait here a moment, I'll go get your money and a set of directions to the Mountain View."

Brant blinked as she closed the door and left him standing on the porch. Mumps? Joey—that was the name Paul had said she'd given the boy—had the mumps? Well, she damn well wasn't going to keep him away when his son was sick! He opened the door and walked into the lodge.

Hearing the slightly uneven footsteps, Jessie glanced over her shoulder and frowned. "You really didn't need to come inside," she said, watching him walk toward her. "This will only take a moment." In the light, she noticed he had a limp, not an extreme one, but noticeable. He was a big man. She judged him to be a little over six feet tall. His face was too angular to be considered handsome, but it was interesting. A lock of dark brown hair had fallen onto his forehead and he combed it back with his fingers. An uneasiness stirred within her. The fact that she and Joey were alone in the inn hit her full force.

Brant saw the anxiety flicker in her eyes. For a moment he was afraid she might have recognized him. But that was ridiculous. He saw her easing around the counter and realized she was heading for the baseball bat she kept hidden there in case it was needed. It was interesting that she sensed danger from him, he thought. That wasn't what he wanted. He smiled reassuringly and held up his free hand in a sign of peace. "I've already had the mumps. A full-blown case. I distinctly recall my sister calling me a chipmunk face. It's perfectly safe for me to stay here."

Jessie continued to watch him guardedly. His smile was pleasant and he seemed harmless enough. It suddenly dawned on her she'd been unnerved by the lock of hair that had fallen on his forehead and the way he had combed it back with his fingers. The action reminded her of a man she never wanted to see again. But Brant Mallery was strikingly handsome with a manner that could charm the fuzz off a peach. The man facing her was neither handsome nor gushing with charm. She was letting old memories cloud her reason. "The inn is scheduled for repairs. I'm going to be doing some painting—" she began, by way of explaining that it really was impossible for him to stay.

He arched his back in an awkward stretch to emphasize his fatigue. "I'm afraid I'll fall asleep at the wheel if I have to drive another foot," he interrupted gruffly. "Couldn't you let me stay at least for the night? I'll pay for the room here and the room at the Mountain View."

Jessie had to admit he did look exhausted. And the thirty miles to Mountain View was over some pretty winding road.

Seeing her weaken, he pressed his point. "You wouldn't want my blood on your hands, would you?"

"No," she conceded. She would have preferred to send him on his way. In spite of the fact that she realized she was allowing images from the past to taint her opinion of this stranger, she still felt uneasy. However, she wouldn't be responsible for his being in an accident. Relenting, she made a quick call to Mountain View to tell them that he wouldn't be coming but that he would pay for the room and wanted them to hold it for him for tomorrow. Hanging up, she reached for a key. Suddenly realizing what room she had chosen, she rehung the key. Even after three years she still remembered which room Brant Mallery had occupied. She didn't want her guest to use that room tonight. Taking down a key for a room as far from hers and Joey's as possible, she handed it to him and slid the registration book toward him.

While he signed, she moved around the desk and started to pick up his suitcase.

"I can carry that," he said, reaching for it at the same time.

As their hands brushed, a warm tingling sensation raced up Jessie's arm and she jerked away. She'd felt that only once before and she didn't want to ever feel it again. She wished she could send Mr. Adams on his way. He'd be leaving first thing in the morning, she reminded herself and turned her attention to the luggage. "I noticed you limping when you came in. You really shouldn't be carrying anything heavy with an injured leg or ankle, especially up a flight of stairs," she said as he lifted the suitcase.

He glanced down at his leg and an impatient anger played across his face. "It's an old automobile-accident injury. It may not work as well as it used to, but it's strong enough."

Jessie frowned at herself. Clearly she had touched a raw nerve. "I'm sorry," she apologized.

"Don't be," he replied coolly. *At least not about the leg. But you do owe me an apology for keeping our son a secret,* he added mentally.

Reminding herself that most men, and obviously her guest, didn't like to have their physical prowess questioned, she led the way up the stairs and to his room. As soon as he entered, she bid him good-night and went to her own room.

Joey's room adjoined hers through a connecting bathroom. After changing into her nightgown, she went in to check on him. He was still sleeping peacefully. Very gently she brushed a lock of hair from his forehead. She had been foolish to think a wealthy, high-powered businessman like Brant Mallery would have been interested in her for very long. For him it had been lust, not love, that had gotten him to the altar. Hurt and anger filled her. Why was he on her mind so much today? He lived in his world and she lived in hers, and if she had anything to do with it, their paths would never cross again.

A sudden rush of fear swept over her. It was not a new fear, just one she tried to keep buried. What if their paths *did* cross and he discovered he had a son? For the millionth time, she told herself he wouldn't care. He'd made it clear that she could never fit into his world. He certainly wouldn't want her son. But Joey was also his son, and men were unpredictable where their children were concerned. "Well, he will never take you away from me," she promised, tucking Joey's blanket more securely around him.

Returning to her own room, she raked her fingers anxiously through her hair. *Stop worrying!* she ordered herself. *You're making mountains out of molehills.* Brant Mallery had severed all ties to her. He'd made it clear he wanted nothing to do with her ever again. It was having the inn vacant that was bringing back the memories. Not exactly vacant, she reminded herself. An image of her guest entered her mind. There was something disturbing about him. Familiarly disturbing. The way he had brushed back the lock of hair, the way the brown of his eyes changed subtly to a deeper sort of pleading shade when he was trying to convince her to allow him to remain. Brant's eyes had done that.

Jessie scowled. She was letting her imagination and her memories get the best of her. Her guest most certainly wasn't Brant Mallery and he was only staying the night. Tomorrow he would be leaving and she would probably never see him again. Forcing Mr. John Adams from her mind, she closed her eyes and fell into a restless sleep.

Brant lay in his bed, staring into the darkness around him. The lodge was exactly as he remembered it—a comfortable, cozy haven for weary travelers. He had smelled the delicious lingering odor of the fire that had been burning in the fireplace before his arrival, and the dark, highly polished wood-planked floors gave the place a sturdy look that suggested it would stand forever. Mentally he traveled to the dining room. When Jessie had guests, there was a fire in the fireplace to greet them in the morning and ward off the chill of the mountain air. Then

there was Jessie herself. He ticked off the years. She
was twenty-eight now, although she still didn't look
a day over twenty. But in subtle ways she had
changed. She was more guarded in her actions and
her smile wasn't as quick. He'd done that, he knew,
but he'd had his reasons and at the time they'd been
damn good ones!

Regret suddenly washed over him. If he could turn
back the clock, do things differently, maybe she
would still be his. A twinge of pain shot up his leg
and he cursed under his breath. Wishes belonged in
fairy tales. He lived in the real world.

He didn't doubt that he had lost Jessie for good.
But he wasn't going to give up his son. She had the
right to be angry and hurt, but she did not have the
right to keep Joey from him.

Chapter Two

Jessie awoke to the sounds of Joey fussing unhappily. She forced herself out of bed and, glancing at the clock, pulled on her robe. It was 3 a.m. Groaning, she went through the bathroom into Joey's room. He was standing in the corner of his crib. When he saw her in the light streaming in from the bathroom, he stretched out his arms toward her.

A soft smile immediately replaced her tired frown. Remembering something Mr. Adams had said, she found herself thinking that the swollen side of the little face did resemble a chipmunk's stuffed pouch. She lifted her son out of the bed and gave him a hug as she crossed the room to switch on the light. She kissed him on the forehead to test his temperature. He still felt warm.

His diaper was wet, too. She'd just about had him potty trained when he'd gotten the mumps, but she'd decided it was best to stop until he was well again. He let out an unhappy yelp when she laid him back in his crib.

"Got to change you, sugar," she explained patiently.

He looked at her grudgingly, but didn't yelp again.

She had just discarded the wet diaper and was securing the dry one in place when a knock sounded on the door, followed immediately by the door swinging open.

"Is everything all right?" Brant asked, entering the room and moving toward the crib in long strides.

"Everything is fine," Jessie assured him, startled by the intrusion. "I'm sorry if we disturbed you. I thought I'd put you in a room far enough down the hall that you wouldn't hear us." Her guest was dressed in slacks and a shirt. The tired lines in his face were etched even deeper than before and she had the impression he hadn't slept at all. But what really rattled her was her acute awareness of his masculinity and the way his presence seemed to fill the room.

Brant didn't inform her he'd left his door wide open and he'd lain there dressed and ready to rise at the first sound from the child. "I'm a light sleeper," he said instead as his gaze fixed on the boy. Brown

eyes identical to his own watched him with open
curiosity. He smiled. His sister had been right about
the resemblance to a chipmunk. Though at the moment, Joey looked as if he only had one pouch full.
"Hi, fella," he said. His arms ached to reach out and
pick up his child. But one glance at Jessie warned
him that could be dangerous.

With the stance of a mother protecting her young,
she had placed herself between her child and her
guest. Now she stood facing the man with a threat
in her eyes. His white broadcloth shirt stretched
across sturdy-looking shoulders. The sleeves were
rolled up, exposing muscular arms. He seemed much
bigger and stronger than she remembered. "We really are just fine. You should be in your room sleeping," she said with undeniable dismissal.

It took every ounce of control he had, but Brant
made himself back away from the crib. The last thing
he wanted was to frighten her into throwing him out
of the inn. "Sorry, I didn't mean to intrude," he said
gruffly.

Jessie stood protectively in front of the crib until
he was gone. Hearing his footsteps moving off down
the hall, she crossed the room, closed the door and
locked it. "You're overreacting," she told herself.
There had been times when other guests, grandmoth-
ers especially, had come knocking on Joey's door at
night when he'd awakened. "I've just never had a

man come check before,'' she murmured, looking for a reason for the sudden apprehension that filled her.

You know what your real problem is? she chided herself as she gave Joey medicine for his fever. *You've lost the ability to trust any man who tries to infringe on your private life.*

"Well, I've got good reason," she muttered.

An hour later she had just rocked Joey back to sleep and had laid him in his crib when the buzzer in her room sounded.

Mentally she ran through the list of her preregistered guests. All were accounted for and she knew she'd put up the No Vacancy sign. She was exhausted and tempted to ignore whomever was at her front door. The buzzer sounded again. This time it continued. The caller was leaning on it. It was going to wake up Joey.

"This had better be one gigantic emergency," she muttered under her breath, hurrying down the stairs. Switching on the hall light, she looked through the curtained window on the door. Chase Murdock, one of the locals who made his living working as a lumberjack, stood there grinning down at her. She flung open the door, then glared up at him. "Get your thumb off that buzzer!" She could smell the whiskey on his breath. He'd made subtle passes at her over the years, but then, he made passes at anything in a skirt. She'd never expected him to show up on her doorstep.

"Got to thinking about your being up here all alone," he said, his speech slightly slurred.

Her scowl deepened. "What you should be thinking about is your wife and kids."

He chuckled. "You look real cute when you're angry."

"Go home, Chase," she ordered. Stepping back, she started to slam the door but he stepped forward, easily holding it open.

"Now that ain't friendly," he drawled, his grin becoming more of a leer.

Jessie decided that reasoning with him would do no good, and being subtle was definitely out of the question. "You'd better leave now or your wife is going to find out about your being here," she threatened bluntly.

His mouth formed a little-boy pout. "Now, Jessie, you wouldn't do a thing like that."

"Yes, I would," she assured him.

The pout became even more exaggerated. "She doesn't understand me. And she's got one hell of a temper."

Jessie regarded him dryly. "I think she understands you just fine. Now go home." Again she tried to close the door; again he stopped her.

Taking a step inside, he smiled mischievously.

"How about just one little kiss?" he coaxed. "You might even like it. This celibate life you've been leading has got to be boring."

"I like my life just the way it is." Jessie began to back toward the registration desk. She was fairly certain Chase was harmless—but he *had* been drinking. Just to be safe, she'd get the baseball bat.

He guessed her ploy. Kicking the door closed with the heel of his boot, he caught up with her in two quick strides. He captured her by the arm, then jerked her up against him. "You don't need that bat. I came here to make love, not war." He grinned. "Come on, Jessie, just one little kiss."

She tried to pull free, but his grip was like iron. He captured her other arm and held her pinned in front of him. For the first time, she realized just how large and strong he was. Standing better than six feet tall, he carried double her weight and all of it muscle. He was, however, afraid of his wife. She was a tiny little thing but full of fire, with a temper to match her red hair. "I'm not kidding, Chase. You'd better leave now or I'll call Iris," Jessie warned.

The pout returned to his face. "That ain't neighborly." Determination glittered in his eyes. His face moved toward hers.

"I'm warning you, Chase, you'd better let go." Jessie was scared now. Chase was being much more persistent than she had thought he would be. Her body tensed and she prepared to drive her knee into his groin. At the same time, she filled her lungs with air. If the kick didn't work, she was going to start screaming. For the first time during this long night she was glad she had a guest at the inn.

Suddenly a muscular arm wrapped itself around Chase's neck. Startled, the logger released his grip on Jessie. She stumbled back, catching a chair to keep from falling.

Her vision blocked by Chase's bulk, and intent on her struggle with him, Jessie hadn't seen or heard her boarder's approach. Now he held Chase captive, one arm around his neck and the other bending his right arm at a painful angle behind his back.

"What...? Who...?" Chase gasped as he struggled uselessly against the iron grasp.

"You ought to pick on someone your own size," Brant growled.

Fear showed in Chase's eyes. "You're choking me," he complained in a childish whine, using his free hand to try to pull Brant's arm away from his neck. It was a futile effort. "Look, I didn't know Jessie had already found someone to keep her company."

"Mr. Adams is not keeping me company," Jessie snapped. "He's a guest."

"Whatever you say," Chase agreed readily. "Just let go of me."

"Apologize to the lady," Brant demanded.

"Sorry, Jessie. Guess I had a little too much to drink. You know me. I can't hold my liquor. I didn't mean any harm," Chase blurted out.

Continuing to hold the man captive, Brant looked at Jessie. "You want to call the sheriff and press charges?"

The fear in Chase's eyes turned to panic. "Hey, there's no need for that. I give you my word, I'll never bother Jessie again."

"I'm not interested in being the center of a lot of unpleasant gossip," Jessie said tightly, refusing Brant's suggestion that she call the sheriff. She didn't add that she'd already had that experience when her husband of four days had asked for a divorce. Her gaze narrowing, she glared at Chase. "But from now on, you'd better stay on the opposite side of the street from me. If you ever come near me again even to say so much as a polite hello, I'm going to tell your wife what happened here tonight," she promised.

"You have my word," he swore.

Brant released him. "Get out of here."

Chase glanced sheepishly at Jessie. "I'm real sorry," he apologized again. His gaze shifted to Brant and he paled at the anger he saw on the man's face. With barely a nod, he scurried out of the inn.

Brant's gaze turned to Jessie. She looked pretty shaken. "You all right?" he asked.

Jessie nodded. "Thanks."

A part of him wanted to shake her while another part wanted to take her in his arms and comfort her. But holding her would only lead to trouble for both of them. The anger won. "Don't you know better than to open the door to a drunk in the middle of the night?" he demanded curtly.

Jessie's back stiffened. "I do now."

Brant's gut twisted when he thought of what might have happened. "You shouldn't be here alone," he said.

Jessie's jaws clenched. There had been a time when she'd thought she would never be alone again. "I don't need you to preach to me. I've learned my lesson, Mr. Adams. In the future I'll answer the door with the baseball bat in my hand."

Brant glared at her. Didn't she realize how close she had come to being harmed? He'd felt the logger's strength. Jessie couldn't have fought him off if the man had demanded more than a kiss. "Learning lessons the hard way can be dangerous," he pointed out.

"I know," she replied dryly, remembering another time when she'd paid dearly for an impulsive act. "But it seems to be a habit I have." Shoving the memories of the past into the dark recesses of her mind, she walked to the front door and locked it. She turned back to face him and made a waving motion toward the stairs with her arm. "I'm tired, Mr. Adams. Shall we return to our rooms?"

The tone of her voice told him she wanted this discussion ended. Brant bit back another admonition about her being more careful. He didn't want to make her angry with him. But as he preceded her up the stairs, he promised himself that he'd see she was protected in the future.

As they reached the second-floor landing, Jessie broke the heavy silence now hanging between them. "I plan to sleep as long as Joey does," she informed her guest. "If you want to leave in the morning before we wake up, just put your key on the desk. And consider the night's lodging free. I owe you."

Brant thought of the child he'd been allowed to glimpse only briefly. He had no intention of leaving, but now wasn't the time to tell her that. "Thanks," he replied stiffly, adding a gruff "good night" as he continued down the hall.

Entering her room, Jessie closed the door then leaned against it. She was trembling. It was a delayed fear reaction. "He's right. You were really stupid to open that door!" she berated herself. Straightening away from the door, she headed toward Joey's room to check on him before going back to bed. "Another lesson learned," she informed her image in the mirror as she passed through the bathroom. "I just wish I could stop learning them the hard way."

In his room, Brant discarded his clothes and climbed into bed. He wanted to kill the logger for touching Jessie. But even more, he wanted her in his arms. An aching filled him as he remembered making love with her. She'd been so warm, so giving. At first, she'd been nervous and he'd been pleasantly surprised to discover she was a true innocent.

Closing his eyes, he recalled how her body had ignited beneath his touch. It had been difficult to go slowly, but he had forced himself. It had been worth it for both of them. Afterward, she had lain in his arms kissing him lightly on the chest. "You have the most beautiful body," she'd said with a satisfied sigh, and he'd laughed softly.

Pushing the memory to the back of his mind, Brant scowled. Again he found himself wishing that his life with Jessie could have taken a different path, one that would have let them stay together. But the past was gone forever. Everything was changed now. There could never be a future for him with Jessie. *You're here to claim your rights as a father and nothing more,* he told himself firmly.

The next morning when Jessie awoke she discovered bruises on her arms left by Chase Murdock's fingers. A frown creased her brow. Chase had better not cross her path again.

Joey's whimpering brought her back to more immediate concerns. She dressed quickly in jeans and a sweater, then went into his room. She changed his diaper, put a fresh pair of heavy-footed pajamas on him and carried him downstairs. Passing the desk, she noticed that the key for John Adams's room wasn't there. She had hoped he would be gone. She was feeling somewhat embarrassed about facing him this morning. Opening that door *had* been foolish.

She set Joey in his high chair, then started the coffee perking and made some baby cereal. Joey wasn't able to swallow anything solid, but she hoped he could get some of this soft mushy stuff down.

She was beginning to spoon the cereal into his mouth when the kitchen door opened. Glancing over her shoulder, she saw her guest enter. "Good morning, Mr. Adams," she said in her best innkeeper tone. "I hope you slept well."

"Fairly well," he replied, leaning against the wide center counter and watching her spoon food into the toddler's mouth—*his son's* mouth. He'd never seen a cuter child. A soft smile spread over his face. Of course, he was prejudiced.

"As soon as I feed Joey, I'll make you some breakfast before you leave," Jessie said, half wishing that he'd decline, say he should be on his way. His presence made her tense. She told herself it was embarrassment even though he hadn't mentioned the incident with Chase. When he didn't make any move to leave, she nodded toward the coffeepot. "Help yourself. There are mugs in the cabinet above it."

"Thanks." Pouring himself a cup of coffee, Brant continued to watch the mother and child. A sense of having been cheated swept over him. He should have been part of the baby's life from the moment he was born. His smile became a judgmental frown. "I thought there was a vaccine for the mumps."

Jessie heard the accusation in his voice, and the hairs on the back of her neck bristled. Men! They always thought they could do everything better. Aloud she said tersely, "There is and he had it. Obviously it didn't take."

Brant was annoyed at himself. He wanted her cooperation. Questioning her ability as a mother wasn't going to earn him that. "I didn't mean to sound critical," he apologized. "Guess I'm still a bit tired."

Jessie took a calming breath and chided herself for overreacting. He had merely been making conversation. That was no reason to bite his head off. "I want to thank you again for what you did last night," she forced herself to say. It was embarrassing to mention his rescue, but it was the polite thing to do.

The memory of seeing Chase manhandle Jessie came sharply to his mind. "Don't you have someone who could come here to stay with you?" he asked. He knew she didn't have any close relatives and her parents were both dead. But surely Jessie had someone she could turn to in times of trouble. The thought that it might be a man caused a sour taste in his mouth.

Jessie frowned. "I appreciate your concern, but I've been taking care of myself, on my own, for several years now. Last night was the first time anything like that has ever happened. And it's going to be the last. If I ever open my door again that late at night, I'll be prepared."

Brant scowled into his coffee. She had to be one of the most stubborn women he'd ever known. However, this conversation had paved the way for questions he wanted answers to. He had to know what she was telling people about him. Even more important, what was she telling Joey? "What about your child's father? Where is he?" he asked.

Jessie's back tensed. She didn't like talking about Brant. She spent a great deal of energy trying never to think of him. "We're divorced. He lives in another state."

"But I suppose he gets up here to see Joey fairly often," Brant persisted, adding sharply, "any man would want to spend time with his son."

A shaft of guilt ran through Jessie. But then, she had no reason to believe Brant Mallery would want to have anything to do with his son. "Some would and some wouldn't," she replied stiffly.

Brant fought to control his anger. Obviously she

classified him as a "wouldn't." But she had been the one to make that decision, and she didn't have that right.

Joey was losing interest in the food. Jessie breathed a sigh of relief. Mr. Adams was setting her nerves on edge. Now she could feed him and send him on his way. "Would you like eggs with bacon, ham, sausage, or any combination of the above?" she offered.

"Eggs and ham sounds good," he replied. He'd seen through her polite demeanor and knew she wanted him to leave. Well, he was just going to have to change her mind.

"And how do you want your eggs?" she asked, lifting Joey out of his chair. Propping the kitchen door open on her way, she carried the child into the dining room.

Forcing himself to remain in the kitchen, Brant watched her as she put Joey on the floor, then opened a playpen and set the child inside among a clutter of toys. He wanted to hold the boy so badly it hurt. "Scrambled," he answered.

Returning to the kitchen, Jessie glanced back to make certain she had a clear view of her son while she cooked.

"He doesn't seem too sick," Brant observed, watching Joey playing with a brightly colored ball.

"I think he's mostly just uncomfortable with the

swelling," she replied, with thoughtful concern. "He only has a slight fever and he actually ate fairly well."

Brant felt a rush of relief. Forcing his attention away from the boy, he insisted on helping prepare the meal. He didn't want her to think he needed to be waited on. That wouldn't get him an invitation to remain.

It wasn't until they were seated in the dining room and eating that he broached the subject of his remaining at the inn.

"To be honest with you, Mrs. Mallery," he began simply, "I like being here. I was looking for a place that was quiet, without too many people. I was wondering if I might stay. I'd be willing to pay double the going rate."

Jessie had to admit that the income would be welcome. This closing was going to cut into her savings. Mr. Adams was already exposed to Joey, and he said he'd already had the mumps. As she lifted her head to meet his gaze, the boyishly coaxing expression on his face sent a warmth spreading through her. Only one other man had ever been able to affect her so strongly with a mere look. A sudden feeling of déjà-vu shook her and an uneasiness filled her. Her instincts seemed to be warning her that it would be best if she sent Mr. Adams on his way. Her savings could carry her through. "As I tried to explain when you arrived, my cook and maid are both gone. They won't be back until the inn reopens. I wanted to use these two weeks to do some extra cleaning, plus a few repairs and spend some time with my son. I really hadn't planned on having a guest.''

Our son, Brant corrected mentally. The simple approach hadn't worked. It was time to do something a little more dramatic. Normally he would consider it caddish to play on a woman's sympathy, but he was fighting for his son. ''I can eat at one of the local restaurants,'' he said, discarding the notion that a cook was necessary. ''The truth is, I need some time alone to get my life back in order. The accident that caused my limp cost me my wife and child.''

Jessie caught the bitterness in his voice and saw his gaze become guarded. Obviously he didn't like to let the depth of his feelings show. She felt a sharp jab of sympathy for him. She didn't even want to imagine how she would feel if anything should ever happen to Joey. And, she reminded herself, she did owe a debt of gratitude to Mr. Adams. It was ridiculous to allow the pain of the past to cause her to act callously. ''You can stay,'' she conceded, still not certain this was wise but unable to turn him away. ''And at half the regular rate, because I can't promise that you'll be comfortable.''

''Thanks.'' Brant focused his attention on his food to prevent her from seeing the triumph in his eyes. ''I'm sure I'll be very comfortable.''

Chapter Three

Jessie awoke with a sharp pain in her neck. This couch was definitely not made for sleeping, she decided, shifting herself into a sitting position.

After breakfast, her guest had gone for a walk into town. She'd cleaned up the kitchen, then moved Joey, playpen and all, into the lounge area. While Joey played with his toys, she'd begun to push the furniture to the center of the room and prepare the walls for painting. But when Joey had fallen asleep, she'd given in to her own fatigue and lain down on the couch and dozed.

When she glanced toward the playpen, her whole body jarred to life. Joey wasn't there! Panic swept over her. He couldn't have gotten out on his own!

Jumping to her feet, she tried to think. Then she heard the giggle from upstairs.

Taking the steps two a time, she reached Joey's room in seconds. The door was open and inside was John Adams, standing beside Joey's crib. "So you think that was funny, do you?" the man was saying good-humoredly.

Jessie rushed to the crib. "What do you think you're doing?" she demanded, grabbing up a loosely diapered Joey.

The warm smile on Brant's face became a frown. "I was trying to change him," he replied, furious that she had grabbed his son away from him. The words that would reveal who he was formed on his tongue but died when he saw the fire in her eyes. She reminded him of a she-cat protecting her young. Now was definitely not the time to lay his claim on the boy. He schooled his face into a contrite expression of apology. "When I came in a few minutes ago, he was getting ready to loft a ball at you. You looked so peaceful, I thought I should intervene. I was going to read him a book, but when I lifted him out of his playpen I realized he was wet so I brought him up here to change him."

Jessie took a couple of calming breaths. "Don't ever do that again," she said levelly. "You scared me half to death."

"I didn't mean to frighten you." Mentally, Brant

berated himself for acting without thinking. But when the opportunity arose for him to hold his son, he hadn't been able to resist.

As Jessie's nerves settled, she stood Joey in his crib. He looked worriedly past her to Brant, as if to ask if the man was safe. Seeing the anxiety in his eyes, Jessie said assuringly, "Everything's all right, hon."

Brant winked at him and Joey smiled back. The exchange startled Jessie. It seemed so natural—almost as if the two of them had known one another all their lives. *For some reason you're overreacting to everything these past couple of days,* she scolded herself. *I've just been worried about Joey, and I'm probably still suffering from some residual fear left from my encounter with Chase Murdock last night,* she reasoned. Still, Joey's affinity with her boarder was unexpected. "I'm surprised that Joey let you pick him up and carry him up here," she heard herself saying as she left the crib and went hunting for a fresh pair of pajamas. "He doesn't usually take to strangers so easily."

"Obviously he knew I was someone he could trust," Brant replied.

Jessie glanced over her shoulder. He did have an air about him that made her feel a certain security. It was his size, she decided, remembering how easily he had handled Chase. Unexpectedly, she found herself wondering what it would be like to have those strong, protective arms around her. Shocked by this thought, she scowled at herself. She barely knew Mr. Adams. Hadn't she learned her lesson about being attracted to a man without first getting to know him? As for Mr. Adams, he obviously wasn't interested in her as a woman. He'd kept his distance and made no remarks that could be construed as passes. And that was the way she wanted it, she told herself firmly.

But where Joey was concerned, Mr. Adams was not as coolly reserved, she noticed. There was tenderness on his face when he looked at her son, and then she remembered that he'd said he'd lost a child, as well as his wife. Again she felt a strong surge of sympathy for her guest. Finding the fresh, dry pair of pajamas, she returned to the crib. Joey's diaper was on a little too loosely and, laying him down, she started to tighten it.

"You'd better be careful," Brant warned with a crooked smile.

Glancing toward him, Jessie saw the wet spot on his shirt. "Boys can be a little dangerous," she said, matching his crooked smile with one of her own.

How well he remembered that smile. The memory of it had carried him through some rough times.

The sudden warmth in his eyes caused Jessie's breath to catch.

Damn! Brant cursed himself, his gaze becoming

guarded. There was no future for him and Jess. It was best if he kept his distance.

Jessie watched the cool mask descend over his features. If he had worn a sign around his neck that said, "Don't get too close," the message couldn't have been any clearer. Obviously he was still in such deep mourning for his wife that even having a friendly relationship with another woman made him feel guilty. Actually she preferred it this way. Her unexpectedly strong response to the man made her uneasy. Returning her attention to Joey, she felt a little ashamed of her behavior when she'd entered the room. "I'm sorry I was so hostile a few minutes ago," she apologized. Then she added, "Joey and I only have each other. Sometimes I can be a bit overprotective of him."

He couldn't fault her for trying to be a good mother. "I shouldn't have taken him without your permission," he said gruffly. But her remark about her and Joey being alone in the world rankled. That had been her choice—a choice she'd had no right to make. "I still find it hard to believe that Joey's father doesn't take more interest in him. He's a very likable child."

Again Jessie felt a nudge of guilt. "If you'll change your shirt, I'll rinse it out for you," she offered, refusing to discuss the subject.

A fresh wave of anger washed over Brant as she

finished changing Joey and the boy stood up and smiled brightly at him. She had robbed him of the first two years of his son's life. "I'll go change now." He forced himself to leave the room before he said something he might regret. This matter had to be handled delicately.

Jessie picked up Joey and carried him downstairs. She moved his playpen into the dining room and sat him in it. Then, after propping open the door of the kitchen, she began to search through the freezer for a container of her homemade soup. But she couldn't force from her mind the questions that were taunting her. Ever since Joey had been born, she had worried about what she would tell him when he was old enough to ask about his father. How would she explain to him why she had never told his father about his existence? "I'll just tell him the truth," she stated aloud.

"Tell what truth to whom?"

Startled, Jessie twisted around to discover that her boarder had entered the kitchen carrying his soiled shirt. He was studying her with that guarded expression she was getting used to seeing on his face. "I was having a private conversation with myself," she replied stiffly. "It's not polite for you to eavesdrop."

"It sounded serious," he persisted, determined to find out who and what had been occupying her mind.

He needed to know if there was a man in her life. That could affect the way he dealt with this situation.

Jessie wasn't ready to talk about Brant with anyone and certainly not with this stranger. "It really isn't your concern," she said with finality.

Like hell it isn't! Brant cursed mentally. But reminding himself he had been here less than twenty-four hours and he had to exercise patience, he let the subject drop. "Can I rinse this shirt out in one of the sinks?" he asked, moving toward the counter where there were two large stainless-steel sinks.

"Just drop it in the first one," Jessie directed. "I'll rinse it out after lunch." Mr. Adams had a way of asking questions that was setting her nerves on edge. But then maybe it wasn't him. Maybe it was her conscience. Either way, she hoped he would disappear for the afternoon. But politeness forced her to offer him lunch. "I'm just warming up some chicken soup. Joey likes the broth. You're welcome to join us if you want."

Brant knew she didn't really want him there. She'd never been a good liar. She always averted her eyes. But what she wanted didn't matter. "Sounds good," he replied.

Jessie forced a smile and began running hot water on the plastic container to loosen the block of frozen soup inside. She was just dumping it into a pan when Joey began to fuss.

"You'd probably feel a lot better if you'd sleep more," she admonished him lovingly, as she went into the dining room and picked him up.

"My mother used to complain that I never slept enough," Brant said, watching her carry Joey into the kitchen. Then he scowled. It wasn't smart to make comparisons just yet.

Balancing Joey on a hip, Jessie checked the heat under the pan. Satisfied it was set correctly, she kissed Joey on the forehead and noted that he was running only a very mild fever. Looking at him more closely, she frowned. His other cheek was beginning to swell. Pretty soon he was going to look like a chipmunk with two full pouches, she mused.

Brant noticed the frown. "Is something wrong?" he demanded.

Startled by the depth of concern in his voice, Jessie swung her gaze to him. "I was just noticing that the swelling is spreading to the other side of his face."

"Maybe you should call the doctor," Brant suggested tensely.

Jessie didn't need him telling her how to take care of her son. "That really isn't necessary. I was expecting it to spread," she replied coolly. Suddenly remembering that he had lost his child, her voice softened. "You must have been a very good father. A bit overprotective maybe, but a good one."

Anger showed in his face. "I never had a chance to spend any time with my son."

Jessie saw the pain that mingled with his anger. "I'm sorry."

Brant's gaze narrowed on Joey. "I like to think that in the future I'll have a second chance."

Bitter regret filled Jessie. Why couldn't Joey's father have been more like Mr. Adams? She had thought he was, she recalled dryly, but she'd been wrong. "I hope you get one," she said earnestly.

I intend to, he replied to himself.

Joey began to fuss and she shifted him to her shoulder as she stirred the soup.

"I could hold him," Brant offered, watching worriedly. "Isn't it dangerous to have him so close to the stove? He could kick the pot over onto you and him."

Mr. Adams's concern was a bit much, Jessie thought. But considering that he'd lost his child, she decided his reactions were understandable. "If you really want to and Joey doesn't mind..." she conceded.

Anxious to hold his son once again, Brant had to control himself to keep from grabbing Joey from her. "You don't mind, do you, guy?" he asked as he gently lifted Joey away from his mother. For a moment the boy looked at him irresolutely, then settled comfortably on the man's arm.

By the time Jessie had the soup heated, Joey had fallen asleep, his little face snuggled into Brant's neck. "Sleep is the best cure for him," she said quietly. "If you don't mind, you could carry him up to his crib and try to lay him down on his stomach without waking him. I can feed him later."

Brant nodded. He hated letting go of the little guy, but he knew she was right. Obeying her instructions, he carried him upstairs. As he laid his son in the crib, Joey made a few gurgling sounds then settled into a peaceful sleep.

Brant waited until he and Jessie were on their way down the stairs before he said worriedly, "I think his temperature was up. He felt fairly warm to me."

She nodded. "He's definitely feeling worse than he did this morning. But that's to be expected with the added swelling."

"I suppose," he muttered, deciding he would take a walk into town that afternoon, find a phone and call his doctor in Boston just to double-check. Where his son's health was concerned he wasn't going to take any chances.

Jessie was dishing up two bowls of soup when the front doorbell rang. "Jessica, where are you?" Philip Reynolds called out as he entered.

Hurrying out to the lobby, she shushed him. "Joey's asleep," she admonished in lowered tones.

"Sorry." His charmingly apologetic smile made

his handsome features even more attractive. Then, his gaze traveling past her to the door of the dining room, he frowned. "Heard you had a guest. I thought you were going to cancel all your reservations."

"I couldn't reach Mr. Adams," she explained defensively. Philip was a tall man with a lean but strong physique. In his expensive business suit he was an imposing figure. As a lawyer, this commanding appearance had proved an asset. Jessie, however, hated the way he could so easily make her feel like a hostile witness being cross-examined.

He raised a quizzical eyebrow in a disapproving manner. "I could have sworn you told me that you had arranged for him to stay at Mountain View."

Philip had shown a romantic interest in Jessie. But when she hadn't encouraged him, he hadn't pushed. He'd been through a difficult divorce, also, and the main thrust of his energies these days was at furthering his career. She had to admit, however, that if she was in the market for a husband, he was a good catch. He was steady, reliable and, at thirty-five, already had one of the must successful law firms in the region. But she didn't like being bullied. "I decided to allow him to remain here," she said levelly.

The frown on Philip's face deepened. "People will talk."

"People always talk," she replied.

Watching the exchange, Brant decided immediately that he didn't like this blond-haired, gray-eyed man who seemed to think he had the right to tell Jessie what she should and should not do. Of course the man wasn't being very successful at the moment, Brant noted. Jessie was a woman with a mind of her own. Still, it rankled him that this man thought he had the right to question her actions. "Name's John Adams," he said stepping forth and extending his hand.

"Philip Reynolds," Philip replied, accepting the handshake as he scrutinized Brant. It was clear from the expression on his face that he didn't regard Jessie's limping boarder as any serious threat. "Nothing personal in what I was saying to Jessica," he explained crisply. "I just don't like to see her at the center of gossip."

"I'm an innkeeper," Jessie snapped. Philip's patronizing tone set her nerves on edge. Normally she simply accepted his manner as part of his personality, but today, in front of Mr. Adams, she found it extremely irritating. "It's my business to provide rooms for people."

"Now, Jessica—" Philip smiled one of his most charming smiles "—I didn't come here to argue. I came here to confirm our date for tonight."

An apologetic flush spread over Jessie's face. "I've been so concerned about Joey and closing down the inn, I totally forgot about the dance at the

Elks' Lodge.'' Regretfully she added, ''I'm really sorry, but I can't leave Joey.''

''I know how seriously you take motherhood,'' Philip said indulgently. ''It's one of the traits I admire in you. But Haddie can look after him. She's raised nine children of her own and had a strong hand in rearing all those grandchildren of hers.''

''I know Haddie is reliable,'' Jessie conceded. Haddie Chambers had come to the inn looking for work when she'd been widowed fourteen years earlier. She'd been the cook there ever since. Jessie considered her more of a friend than an employee, and she knew Haddie adored Joey. Still, she could not bring herself to leave her son when he was ill. ''But Joey's fever is back up and he's beginning to swell on the other side. I couldn't enjoy myself. I'm really sorry.''

''I think you're being too much of a mother hen,'' Philip said with a resigned sigh. ''But there's no sense in your coming to the dance if you're going to spend the evening worrying.'' He glanced at Brant, and his manner became that of a man staking his claim. Returning his attention to Jessie, he gently captured her chin in his hand. He tilted her face upward and placed a light kiss on her lips. ''I'll call you tomorrow.''

Philip Reynolds was not the man to be Joey's stepfather, Brant decided as he watched the lawyer exit.

He knew that Jessie was young and pretty and would eventually remarry, but Philip Reynolds was totally unacceptable. "Is he your steady boyfriend?" he asked with forced casualness as the door closed behind Philip. Brant needed to know just how seriously she was involved before he determined his next move.

"He's the only man I've been dating lately. I suppose you could classify him as that," she replied, only half-cognizant of the conversation. She was still thinking about the kiss. It hadn't been unpleasant. But it hadn't sparked any excitement, either. It had felt bland. All of Philip's kisses felt that way. "He's considered a very good catch," she added, speaking more to herself than to her almost forgotten companion.

"A tuna is a good catch, but you wouldn't want to marry one," Brant remarked dryly.

"No," Jessie admitted. She breathed a tired sigh. "But sometimes I get lonely." Suddenly she flushed scarlet as she realized she had spoken aloud.

Brant cupped her chin in his hand and turned her face up to his. His eyes flashed with a challenge. "But you are not in love with him."

His touch was sending currents of heat rushing through her, and her heart began to pound wildly. It occurred to her that *his* kiss would not be the least bit bland. Suddenly she was furious at the thoughts

filling her mind. Hadn't she learned her lesson about
staying away from strangers? "No, I'm not in love
with Philip," she admitted curtly, "but maybe it's
safer that way." Jerking free of his touch, she started
toward the dining room. "Our soup is going to get
cold if we don't eat now," she threw over her shoulder, her tone warning him that the subject of Philip
was to be dropped.

Following her, Brant frowned. Jessie had changed.
She'd become cynical about love, and that was his
fault. His jaw tensed. But cynical or not, she wasn't
going to marry Philip Reynolds or anyone else whom
he didn't approve of for Joey's stepfather.

Seating himself at the table, he decided it was time
to lay some groundwork. He had to get her to tell
him about herself before he revealed information she
wouldn't expect him to know. "I have to admit I'm
a little surprised to find that this place belongs to
such a young woman—or are you just the manager?"

Jessie shifted her attention from her soup to her
guest. If he was getting ready to make a pass at her,
she was throwing him out. She could still feel a lingering warmth from where he had cupped her chin;
she'd had enough experience with animal magnetism
to last a lifetime. But his expression was purely one
of polite interest. She was overreacting again, she
chided herself. "I own it," she replied. "My parents

bought the inn right after they were married. I was raised here."

"And now they've retired and left you to run the place," Brant prodded with an easy smile. He hated causing her the pain the subject of her parents would bring up, but it was necessary. It wouldn't do for him to make a slip and admit he knew she was an orphan if she hadn't already told him.

In spite of the years that had passed since her parents' deaths, Jessie still missed them. "They're both dead," she replied stiffly.

"I'm sorry." Her obvious lingering grief caused a sharp jab of guilt. He would have liked to move on to a less painful subject, but he could not pass up this opportunity to try to make her understand how she was depriving Joey by not sharing him. "For you and for Joey. I remember my maternal grandparents. I could nearly always count on them to come to my aid when my parents were angry with me. Seems I wasn't exactly the best-behaved kid on the block."

Jessie studied his chiseled features. There was a strong will in the set of his jaw, and she caught the momentary flash of mischief in his eyes when he mentioned his childhood. "I can believe that," she said with a thoughtful smile. The smile suddenly became a frown, and she returned her attention to her food. For a moment, she'd found herself picturing Mr. Adams as a dirt-smeared little boy, and the picture had caused a strong tug on her heart. The last thing she needed was to fall for another stranger.

Brant schooled his expression into one of friendly interest. He knew he was treading on thin ice, but he wasn't willing to stop now. "What about Joey's paternal grandparents? Are they still living? If so, I'll bet they dote on him. He's about the cutest little guy I've ever seen."

Again Jessie felt a surge of guilt. Then she reminded herself that Brant Mallery's family probably didn't even know he had been married. "The mistake," as he had referred to their marriage in his letter, was something he had no doubt kept secret. "I believe Joey's grandmother is still living," she replied tightly, remembering that Brant had told her his father had died several years ago, but his mother was still alive—at least at the time they were married. "But we never see her. It was an unpleasant divorce." Her appetite suddenly gone, she rose and carried her dishes into the kitchen. She had expected the anger she felt toward Brant to have lessened through the years, but it hadn't. The feeling of abandonment was stronger than ever.

"I didn't mean to open old wounds."

Glancing over her shoulder, Jessie saw that her guest had followed her into the kitchen. "It's all right," she replied, adding with a self-effacing grimace, "I thought they had healed more thoroughly."

I had hoped they had, too, Brant thought worriedly. This could mean real trouble when she found out who he really was. Aloud he said coaxingly, "Want to talk about it?"

"No," was her firm response. After putting her dishes in the dishwasher, she turned to find him studying her, his face shuttered. He seemed to know just where all of her raw edges were, she thought, and again she wished she had sent him on his way. "I hope you don't mind finishing your lunch alone," she said. "I've got work to do." Without waiting for a response, she skirted around him and out of the kitchen.

She had spread plastic sheeting over the furniture she had moved into the center of the lounge and was beginning to wipe the base moldings when she heard Mr. Adams's uneven stride.

"I was wondering if I could be of some help," he offered, coming to a halt in front of her.

From her kneeling position on the floor, her eyes traveled up along the legs of his expensive tan slacks which did not hide the muscular strength beneath them, to his flat abdomen and broad shoulders. A womanly appreciation of his masculine physique stirred within her. Granted he wasn't perfect. His bad leg caused him to stand with a mild tilt. But even so, there was no impression of weakness about him. Feeling her pulse suddenly beating more rapidly, she scowled at herself. Thoughts like that were only going to get her into trouble, she knew, wondering what kind of insanity was guiding her mind. She hadn't been interested in any man since Brant had left her. Now, suddenly, in spite of her efforts not to, she was thinking wanton thoughts about a total stranger. "You're supposed to be on vacation," she replied, returning her attention to her sponge and rinsing it out. "You should be relaxing."

"I'm not used to sitting around idle," he countered.

Considering the unwanted reactions she was having to this man, Jessie was in no mood to have him around, idle or otherwise. "And I'm not used to having guests doing maintenance work," she rebutted. "Thanks for the offer, but I can handle this on my own."

Brant was trying to think of some way to persuade her to let him help her when he heard the sounds of a baby waking.

"I figured he wouldn't sleep too long," Jessie muttered as she dropped the sponge into the water. Taking off the rubber gloves she was wearing, she hung them over the side of the bucket and picked up the portable intercom.

A couple of minutes later as she deftly changed Joey's diaper, she heard Mr. Adams going to his room. "Maybe he'll take a nap and stay out of my way for a while," she muttered.

She took Joey down to the kitchen, then reheated the soup and fed him. He didn't eat much, but she hadn't expected him to. The second side of his face was swelling quickly and he was cranky. Deciding that his need for her was more immediate than that of the lounge wall, she started to carry him back to his room.

But as they passed through the lobby, Joey pointed toward the lounge. "Man," he said with interest.

Looking to where her son was pointing, Jessie saw Mr. Adams. He had changed to a pair of faded jeans and was on his hands and knees, washing the woodwork. She moved toward him. "I told you I didn't need any help," she said, embarrassed that a guest was cleaning the inn.

"And I told you I was no good at being idle," he replied.

He had a look in his eyes and a stubborn set to his jaw that reminded her of Joey when her son was determined to have his way. Realizing she was fighting a losing battle, she shrugged. "Suit yourself."

Brant smiled. "Thanks, I will." The smile became a frown as his gaze shifted to the child. "Joey looks worse than he did this morning. Shouldn't you call the doctor?"

"No, I shouldn't," she replied impatiently. On her

own, she worried enough about Joey when he was sick. She didn't need Mr. Adams adding to her anxiety. "There is nothing the doctor can do."

Watching her carry the boy upstairs, Brant warned himself to be careful, not to overreact and arouse Jessie's suspicion. But he still had the urge to call his own doctor in Boston. Controlling it, he forced himself to concentrate on washing the woodwork. He'd expected Jessie to come back downstairs with Joey fairly quickly. When she didn't he began to worry. Finally, he tossed the sponge into the bucket, dried his hands on his jeans, then rose and strode out of the room. He had to know what was wrong.

As he climbed the stairs, he heard Jessie's voice. It was calm and gentle. Forcing himself to move more sedately, he walked quietly down the hall. The door to the child's room was open and, looking inside, he saw Jessie rocking Joey while she read to him from a large picture book.

Suddenly feeling as though she was being watched, Jessie glanced toward the door and saw her guest standing there. "Is something wrong?" she asked.

"No." Brant wasn't certain how to explain his sudden appearance. He said the only thing that came to mind. "I was on my way to my room and heard you reading the story. I wondered how it ended."

"Happily," Jessie replied. Unlike real life, she

added to herself. Watching her guest standing in the doorway, she was filled with a sudden apprehension. A lock of hair had once again fallen on his forehead. It was too familiar. Even worse were the womanly stirrings he evoked in her. One Brant Mallery was enough for any woman to experience in a lifetime. Again she considered asking him to leave and find other lodgings. Then she reminded herself that he had recently lost his wife and child. She couldn't be that callous. Besides, he hadn't made a single advance toward her. In fact, he'd shown little interest in her. It was *her* reactions to *him* that were disturbing, and she was determined to ignore them in the future.

"Man," Joey said, pointing and beginning to squirm out of her lap.

Releasing him, Jessie watched Joey toddle across the room and come to a halt in front of Mr. Adams. Again her son's friendliness toward this stranger surprised her. Joey was normally more cautious and took his time warming up to people.

Holding up the stuffed animal in his hand, Joey said, "Simon."

"He's introducing you to Simon," Jessie explained.

Brant smiled. Squatting so that he could be closer to eye level with the child, he took one of the stuffed animal's arms and shook it gently as he said, "Hello, Simon."

His mission accomplished, Joey turned, toddled back to Jessie and crawled back up into her lap.

"He doesn't introduce Simon to just anyone," she said, watching her guest straighten. The tenderness in his eyes as they continued to rest on Joey startled her. He must be remembering his own child, she thought. An urge to put her arms around him and tell that time would heal his wounds filled her. But time hadn't healed hers. Besides, every instinct warned her that putting her arms around Mr. Adams could be dangerous.

"I'm honored," he replied. He wanted to stay, but he knew he shouldn't. Patience, he ordered himself for the umpteenth time, schooling his face into a polite mask. "Since you've assured me the story has a happy ending, I'll get back to work."

As she listened to his footsteps moving down the hall, Jessie again wondered if she had been wise to allow him to stay. The way he was insinuating himself into her life was having an uneasy effect on her, even if there was nothing personal in his actions. It was the questions he asked, she decided. But they were questions she had asked herself a hundred times before.

There was a grim expression on Brant's face as he descended the stairs. He found himself wishing that he, Jessie and Joey could be a family. Maybe he had made the wrong decision about the divorce. His jaw tensed. No, he had made the right one. There was no future for him and Jessie. A wave of bitterness washed over him. Scowling, he pushed the thoughts of her from his mind. But there *was* a future for him and his son, and he would not give that up.

Chapter Four

During the next few days, Jessie watched her guest and her son grow closer and closer. But where she was concerned, Mr. Adams kept his distance. She did notice that he always had a barbed remark to make about Philip whenever Philip stopped by for a visit. But he never once made a pass at her. It was as if he had constructed an invisible barrier between himself and her.

She told herself that this suited her just fine. He had insisted on continuing to help her with the painting of the inn, and sometimes while they were working together, his hand or shoulder or leg would brush her. In spite of all her efforts to feel nothing, an excitement would stir within her. But she had played with fire once before and been badly burned. She did not want to play with it again.

On the last night of his stay at the inn, Brant lay in his bed unable to sleep. When he had come here, he had planned to reveal his true identity and demand a place in his son's life. Now he wasn't certain how to go about this. He was getting close to Joey. But each time he brought up Joey's father, Jessie's reaction had been hostile. He didn't want the developing closeness with his son to be shattered by her anger. Tossing restlessly, he wished he could stay longer, but he had to get back to his office. He'd been in touch with his secretary, Ester Vales, twice a day, and she knew how to contact him in case of an emergency. But a backlog of work was building on his desk.

Unable to sleep, he threw off the covers and climbed out of bed. Dressing in a pair of slacks and a shirt, but staying barefooted so he wouldn't wake Jessie or Joey, he went downstairs.

Together, he and Jessie had painted the lounge, the lobby, and the dining room. Then they'd cleaned and waxed the hardwood flooring. The place looked great. He smiled as he remembered how she'd fought his help at first. But he'd been persistent and she'd capitulated. She was, however, refusing to accept any money from him for his room. That part didn't matter. He'd already called Paul and altered his will.

He'd make certain she and Joey never needed for anything.

Brant crossed the lobby and headed toward the lounge. Suddenly he came to an abrupt halt. Jessie was there. Silhouetted by the moonlight, she was standing like a statue in front of one of the long front windows. Silently, he stood watching her. He was reminded of another night, a night several years ago—the night he'd proposed. *The past is buried and gone,* he told himself curtly.

Jessie hadn't been able to sleep. She told herself she would be glad when Mr. Adams left the next day. He stirred emotions she didn't want to feel, and he asked questions that kept her nerves on a raw edge. Still, she had been restless. Finally, she had pulled on her robe and wandered downstairs. There was a full moon. Its light streamed into the windows in the lounge, illuminating the room with a dim, eerie glow. A lover's moon, Jessie mused. Loneliness swept over her, and she found herself wanting a man to hold her. Standing, looking out at the wooded landscape, she wondered if maybe she should marry Philip. But it wasn't Philip's image that filled her mind; it was Mr. Adams's. "Thoughts like that will only cause you trouble," she warned herself aloud.

Brant wondered what thoughts she was speaking about. He would liked to have listened longer, but if she turned and found him there it would only cause more friction between them. "I apologize for eavesdropping on another of your private conversations," he said gruffly, breaking his silence.

Startled, Jessie whirled around. Feeling suddenly vulnerable, she checked to make certain her robe was fastened. "I didn't hear you come down the stairs," she said.

"I was trying to be quiet so I wouldn't wake you or Joey," he explained. "I couldn't sleep, so I thought I'd come down here for a little while."

His steady gaze made Jessie self-conscious. "It must be the full moon. I couldn't sleep, either."

She looked so inviting. Brant wanted to stride across the room and take her in his arms. But he was a practical man. That action would serve no good purpose. "At least Joey is getting a good night's sleep," he remarked, forcing himself to remember precisely why he was here.

"Yes," Jessie agreed. She was having a hard time trying not to wonder what it would be like to have Mr. Adams's arms around her. He was a gentle, caring man. She'd seen that in the way he behaved with her son. Turning away from him, she again focused her gaze on the view beyond the window.

"He appears to have survived the mumps without any side effects," Brant persisted, recalling with cynical amusement how he had finally given in to his concern and sneaked into town to call his own doctor. He knew he was being overly protective, but he hadn't been able to stop himself.

"Yes," Jessie replied, wishing just once he would say something to her that didn't involve Joey. Furious with herself for this thought, her jaw tensed.

"And tomorrow, the inn will reopen," Brant finished.

And you'll be leaving, Jessie added silently. She told herself she was glad. His presence had been disquieting. But deep inside, the aloneness she had felt earlier again stirred within her. Determined to ignore it, she said with a forced cheerfulness, "Back to business as usual."

Brant was tempted to keep the conversation on impersonal ground. He didn't like upsetting Jessie. But he had to try one last time to get her to talk about her feelings toward him. For two weeks she had avoided answers to his questions about her son's father, and he had allowed it. But tomorrow he would be leaving, and he needed information to help him decide on his next move. "I'm surprised Joey's father hasn't called in the past two weeks to check on his health."

Jessie's back tightened. Why did John Adams have to constantly bring up the subject of Joey's father? "He didn't know."

"Don't you think you should have told him?" Brant questioned, working hard to keep the accusation out of his voice. "He might have wanted to call Joey and let him know he was thinking about him."

Jessie's jaw trembled. "I doubt that," she said grimly.

"Are you sure you're being fair?"

Bitterness swept over Jessie as she remembered the long nights right after Brant had left. She'd stood at this same window watching, waiting for his return. But he hadn't returned. "Fair?" she said cynically. She had no reason to be "fair" to Brant Mallery. He'd used her and then left without a backward glance.

Brant willed his voice to be calm. "I remember you said it was an unpleasant divorce. But that was between you and your former husband. Do you think it's right to build barriers between Joey and his father?"

Jessie raked a hand through her hair. She didn't know what was right anymore. Joey was growing up. He'd be asking about his father one of these days. What was she going to tell him? "The truth is, Joey's father doesn't even know about him," she admitted.

Brant drew a terse breath. Now they were getting somewhere. "He doesn't know he has a son?"

"When he asked for the divorce, I wasn't aware that I was pregnant," Jessie replied defensively. "When I did realize it, I figured it was none of his

business. He hadn't wanted me. Surely he wouldn't
want my child.''

"Joey is partly his child, too," Brant pointed out,
still fighting to keep his voice level.

Jessie's eyes narrowed in anger. "I prefer to ignore that part."

Time to try another tack, Brant decided. "You said
your parents are dead and you've no close relatives.
What happens to Joey if something happens to you?"

"I have a close friend who has agreed to be his
guardian and raise him. She's a good, kind person,"
she replied.

"Your cook, Haddie Chambers?" Brant guessed.
The woman had called several times to inquire about
Joey and had brought baked goods by three or four
times during the past two weeks.

"Yes," Jessie admitted. "Haddie loves him. She
also knows how to run this lodge and she'll keep it
operating for him until he's old enough to take over,
if that's what he wants to do."

"Haddie isn't young anymore. It's my guess she's
in her mid-fifties," Brant pointed out. "What happens to Joey if she's not able to take care of him?"

"Then Haddie's daughter and her husband will
raise him," Jessie replied. She'd been over this a
million times in her mind. It was the right decision.

Brant was finding it difficult to keep his temper
under control. She had no right to give his son to

strangers to raise. "Those people are not his flesh and blood." He stared at her rigid back. "What are you going to tell Joey about his father?"

Jessie shrugged. "I don't know."

Brant lost control. She was holding his future with his son in her hands. "Are you going to lie to him and tell him that his father's dead?" he demanded harshly. "Or, never giving his father a chance to speak for himself, are you going to tell Joey his father was a bad man who didn't want him?"

The accusation in his voice cut her deeply. He had no right to judge her! Jessie turned to face him. "I won't lie to Joey. Too many people know who his father is. I honestly don't know what I will tell him. But whatever it is, it isn't any of your business."

Oh, yes it is! Aloud he warned, "Whatever you tell him, it had better be the truth, because sooner or later, Joey is going to want to meet his real father."

"I know," she conceded through clenched teeth. This thought had tormented her since Joey's birth. She wondered if, when the moment came for the father and son to meet, Brant Mallery would exert his charm and win his son over with false love, as he had won her, or would he reject him, leaving Joey to feel unwanted? Either way, in the end her son would be hurt. "But it would be better if they never met," she said with conviction.

Brant's jaw tensed. "You can't be certain of that."

Jessie glared at him with self-righteous indignation. "I know the man. You don't. I doubt he is capable of honestly loving anyone." Stalking toward the stairs, she added a terse good-night in a tone that told him this conversation was over.

Watching her in silence, Brant knew he deserved this blow, but she was wrong. The problem was going to be convincing her of that.

"I'm sorry if I overstepped my bounds last night," he apologized the next morning.

Jessie found herself wishing he had let the anger stay between them. She felt safer that way. "I suppose you were thinking of yourself and your child," she said. "I can't blame you for that. But you don't know Joey's father."

He was tempted to tell her that he knew Joey's father very well, but this still wasn't the time. Instead he said, "I'll be coming back this way at the end of the week. I was wondering if I could book a room for the weekend?"

Jessie had been telling herself that she would be glad to be rid of the man. But her stomach did a little butterfly spasm at the thought of his returning. *He's not coming back to see you,* she chided herself. "Of course," she said, and penciled his name in the book.

As he drove away, she stood at the window and watched. Before he had come into her life, she had become complacent, refusing to worry about the future. Now the questions he had raised about Joey tormented her, and this time they refused to go away.

Late that night, she reached a decision. She was going to have to face Brant Mallery. Not only for Joey's sake but for her own. Lying in bed, the aloneness she had felt the night before had returned and, with it, the image of John Adams. She couldn't deny that she was attracted to the man. That he hadn't demonstrated any attraction toward her didn't matter. The feelings he stirred in her were still scary. Her experience with Brant Mallery had left her afraid to trust her own emotions where men were concerned. Grudgingly she admitted that she was afraid to fall in love again. "It's time to face the past and put it behind me," she told herself firmly.

Two days later, Jessie guided her car through the busy traffic just north of Boston. It was midafternoon as she turned into the industrial park that housed Mallery Industries. She had left Joey with Haddie back at the lodge. She wasn't even certain she was going to tell Brant about his son. "I'll play it by ear," she muttered, using the sound of her own voice to give her courage.

Brant Mallery sat drumming the eraser of a pencil on the hard mahogany surface of his desk.

"What next?" Paul asked, watching the younger man with concern. "Do you want me to start drawing up papers demanding your rights to see your son?"

Brant scowled. "I don't want him caught between Jess and me. But I'll be damned if I'm going to give him up." A gentleness suddenly came into his eyes. "He's really something."

Jessie's legs felt weak during the ride up in the elevator to the executive offices of Mallery Industries. As she reached for the handle of the door leading into them, her courage threatened to fail her. Pausing, she made a last quick inspection of the gray business suit she had chosen to wear. The matching four-inch high-heeled shoes added height to her five-foot-five-inch frame, and she'd pulled her hair back into a tight chignon. On the surface, at least, she looked cool and confident. "You've come too far to turn back now," she told herself curtly, and turning the knob, she opened the door and entered.

A large reception room greeted her. To her relief it was empty except for the secretary at the far end guarding the inner sanctum. The name Ester Vales was inscribed on the wooden plate sitting on the woman's desk.

"I would like to see Mr. Mallery," Jessie said, coming to a halt in front of the efficient-looking, gray-haired woman. Jessie had expected someone young and sexy, with a dress cut to reveal well-developed feminine attributes. That would have been more in keeping with the mental picture she had formed of Brant and his life-style during the past couple of years.

Looking up from her typing, Ester smiled politely at the young woman in front of her. "Can I help you?"

"I would like to see Mr. Brant Mallery," Jessie repeated. She knew she should have made an appointment, but she'd decided that surprise was a better tactic. This way he wouldn't have a chance to prepare for their meeting. Recalling his smooth charm, she knew she needed every advantage she could get.

"I'm afraid Mr. Mallery is in conference for the rest of the day." Ester opened her appointment book. "He has an opening tomorrow at ten."

Jessie's gaze shifted to the large double doors behind the woman. "I really need to see him today," she insisted. *Before my courage fails me,* she added silently.

Ester studied the tense-looking young woman in front of her. Trouble, she decided. "If you will just give me your name and state your business, I will set up the appointment for tomorrow," she said sternly.

Jessie shifted her gaze back to the secretary. "Tell

Mr. Mallery that Jessie is here to see him," she said curtly. "And tell him that I will wait out here all night if necessary."

Ester was one of the handful of people who knew about Brant's marriage and divorce. Because Brant trusted her discretion, she had been the one to type his letter and the divorce papers. It had also been necessary for her to know of his ploy as Mr. Adams and the existence of his son. She had spent a lifetime maintaining a polite calm under all sorts of circumstances, but she had not expected Brant's Jessie to suddenly appear in front of her desk. For a moment she hesitated, uncertain of what to do.

"Please give him my message," Jessie insisted.

Ester nodded. Using the phone instead of the open intercom, she buzzed the inner sanctum.

Jessie heard the phone ring in the inner office. So Brant was behind those doors. She knew what she was about to do wasn't polite, but then he certainly hadn't treated her with any deference. Without giving herself a chance to change her mind, she strode past the desk and into the inner sanctum.

Abruptly she froze. The man behind the desk holding the receiver in his hand rose to his feet, a stunned expression on his face. But it wasn't Brant Mallery. It was John Adams. Her gaze shifted to the other man in the room. She recognized him, too. Paul Johnson—he'd spent a couple of days at her lodge a few weeks earlier.

The heavy silence that filled the room was broken by Ester Vales. "I'm sorry, Brant," she said, rushing in behind Jessie. "I didn't know she would burst in like this."

"Brant?" Jessie stared at John Adams. "You're not Brant Mallery."

"Yes, I am," he corrected her, regaining his composure and replacing the receiver. "I was in an accident. I've had plastic surgery. It changed my face."

Fear suddenly caused Jessie to become pale. He knew about Joey. "You've been spying on me."

"I asked Paul to check on you while he was on vacation," Brant explained, moving around his desk and coming toward her. "I wanted to make certain life was treating you well."

"*You* wanted to make certain life was treating *me* well?" Sarcasm etched itself deeply into her features. "Now that's good for a laugh."

Brant's gaze narrowed as he came to a halt in front of her. "And I discovered I had a son you chose not to tell me about."

Her eyes glistened with fury. "Joey is *my* son. You used me and then you deserted me. You have no right to him and you are not going to take him away from me." She wheeled around. She had to get back to Joey!

Fingers like steel closed around her arm, preventing her escape. "No, I'm not going to take him away from you, but we are going to share him." Brant's gaze swung to Paul and then Ester. "Leave us alone. Jessie and I need to talk."

Jessie was too angry and too frightened to be embarrassed by the fact that she and Brant had an audience. "Let go of me or I'll start screaming," she warned, trying to jerk free.

"Mrs. Mallery, Brant doesn't mean you any harm," Paul said in soothing tones, trying to act as peacemaker.

She stopped her struggle to turn and glare at him. "He just wants my son, that's all. Right?"

"Go!" Brant ordered, his voice threatening.

For a moment the lawyer and secretary hesitated. Then, casting worried glances over their shoulders, they obeyed.

As the door closed behind them, Brant released Jessie, then strode to the heavy double doors and locked them. "Now we are going to have a talk."

Jessie took a couple of deep breaths and tried to think. She had been anxious about facing Brant. Discovering he was John Adams was a shock. So far, all of her reactions had been based on fear and anger. What she needed was a cool, clear mind.

"I did not desert you as callously as you believe," Brant began.

"You left four days after we were married. You said you had to get back here to take care of a business matter. While you were gone, I was supposed to arrange for someone to take over the management of the inn. You said you would be back in a couple of days to take me home with you." Bitter tears burned at the back of Jessie's eyes as memories she wanted to keep behind her flooded into her mind. "I waited for you to call. You had said you would call as soon as you got home. When you didn't, I started to worry. So I called your house. I remember the butler asked who I was. I told him my name was Jessie. I didn't know if you had told anyone yet about the marriage, so I didn't give a last name or mention that I was your wife. He informed me that you were unavailable to come to the phone but that he would tell you I called. For two weeks I waited. Nothing. Then your lawyer showed up with a letter saying you'd realized you had made a mistake and you wanted a divorce. That sounds pretty callous to me." The tears burned hotter and she hated herself for wanting to cry. He didn't deserve her tears.

Brant's jaw tensed. "The day I left you, I was in the accident that left me like this."

Jessie stared at him in confusion. "Why wasn't I notified?"

"No one here in Boston knew about us. Remember? I was going to break the news to them when I got home, but I never got home. Instead I was hit by a drunk driving a truck, a very large truck." He paced across the room, coming to a halt in front of the window. Gazing out, he continued grimly, "When I regained consciousness, I had no face, and I was paralyzed from the waist down."

Jessie's jaw trembled as she pictured him in the hospital bed. "You should have had someone call me."

"Why?" He turned to face her and there was bitterness in his eyes. "So you could spend months sitting by the bed of a man who could not be certain he wouldn't end up looking like a freak in a sideshow?" He smiled cynically. "As it turned out, I have a functional face that doesn't frighten people or make them feel sick but it could never be considered handsome."

"You must think I'm a very shallow woman."

Brant raked a hand agitatedly through his hair. "There was more than just my looks to consider. As far as I knew, I might never walk again. I might spend the rest of my life bound to a wheelchair."

Jessie recalled that, as Mr. Adams, Brant had told her he had lost his wife and child because of an accident. He hadn't lost them. He had pushed them away. "I would have come no matter what the outcome," she said stiffly.

"I know. But I couldn't do that to you."

Jessie watched him guardedly. "But what about afterward? When you knew you would walk again, why didn't you come and explain?"

"By then I figured we were better off the way we were. You had your life and I had mine," he replied coolly. It was the truth. Not the whole truth. But it was better this way.

Jessie's stomach knotted so tightly she had to fight to keep from crying out in pain. Self-directed anger filled her as she realized how desperately she had been hoping he would have a good excuse for not contacting her. Even more she had hoped he would confess that he still loved her. Instead he had rejected her a second time. *You stupid fool!* she berated herself. Vividly she recalled how he had kept his distance at the inn when he'd pretended to be Mr. Adams. He hadn't contacted her because he had never been in love with her. Real love did not die so easily. She was a testimony to that. In spite of the hurt she had felt since he'd left her, she would have forgiven him if he'd said he still loved her and wanted her back. *Idiot! Idiot!* she ranted at herself. Lust and restlessness had caused him to marry her. Nothing more. Her back straightened with pride. "You were right. We do both have our own lives now, and it's better if we keep it that way."

She started toward the door. She had never thought

that he could make her hurt like this again. She had to get away.

He reached her before she could get to the door, and his hand again closed around her arm. "It's not as simple as that, Jess. We have a son and I do mean 'we.' I'm going to be a part of my child's life."

Anger hid her pain as she glared up into his face. "I suppose Joey and I should feel honored that he passed your inspection," she sneered. "But he doesn't need a father who wouldn't claim him without coming around first in a disguise to see if he was good enough to be acknowledged."

Brant's hold on her arm tightened painfully. "That is not the reason I passed myself off as John Adams. I wanted to know what was going on. I wanted to know what you were telling Joey and the rest of the people in Oak Valley about me." His jaw twitched with controlled rage. "*And* I wanted to know what right you thought you had to choose not to tell me I had a son."

Jessie matched his fury with her own. "You were the one who set the rules," she reminded him. "You were the one who shut me out of your life, called our marriage a mistake and made it clear through your lawyer that you never wanted to cross my path again. I was merely complying with your wishes."

"Well, I'm changing the rules," he growled.

"You cannot simply walk into people's lives and

run them the way you want.'' Her eyes rested on the hand holding her captive, her expression that of one observing a distasteful insect. "Now let go of me.''

He did as she demanded, then faced her with cool control. He didn't like threatening her, but he had no choice. He had given up too much. He would not give up his son. "I'm going to be a part of my son's life. I'll take you to court if necessary. But for Joey's sake I was hoping we could work out an arrangement without the ugliness of a legal battle.''

A chill of renewed fear shook Jessie. Brant Mallery had a lot of money, and money meant power. "This has all been a shock,'' she said, forcing herself to sound more reasonable. "I need some time to think.''

To her relief Brant nodded. "I'll come up to the inn this weekend and we can talk.'' He drew a deep breath and the anger on his face retreated. "I'm not going to take your son away from you, Jess. But I won't give up my claim to him, either.''

She wished she could believe him. But there was too much at stake. "We'll talk this weekend,'' she repeated.

"And Jess—'' Brant's voice carried a warning "—don't try to take Joey and run. I'll find you.''

The thought had crossed her mind, but she wasn't going to admit that to him. She faced him proudly.

"The inn is my home and Joey's. No threat from you is going to run us out of it."

Brant had always admired her strength. But this time it would be directed against him. "I'm glad to hear that." He walked to the doors and unlocked them. "Until the weekend," he said, opening the door and stepping aside to allow her to leave.

Ester was seated behind her desk. Paul was standing beside it. Both watched silently as Jessie left.

"I'm so sorry she got past me," Ester apologized to Brant the moment the reception room door closed behind Jessie.

"It's all right," he assured her, but his expression was grim. He had wanted more time as Mr. Adams before Jessie found out the truth about his identity.

"Can I take it as a good sign that the two of you didn't part screaming at one another?" Paul asked.

"I don't know," Brant replied honestly. Returning his attention to Ester, he said, "Get Howard Green on the phone for me. He's at Jessie's inn." Then, turning back to Paul, he nodded toward his office. "Come in. We need to work out an agreement I can present to her this weekend."

A few minutes later, Brant's private line rang. "Why didn't you tell me Jess was coming to Boston?" he demanded as soon as he recognized the voice on the other end.

Howard Green frowned at the receiver. He'd never

heard Brant Mallery so angry. "Because I didn't know. She left the boy here and she didn't take a suitcase. I saw her toss one of those small gym bags into the car, but I figured she was just going shopping for the day and maybe planned to stop for an aerobics class or something. You didn't tell me I was supposed to keep track of all of her movements. You said I was to hang around the inn and make sure she and the boy weren't bothered by any of the guests or locals. What happened?"

"She came to see me," Brant growled. "Let me know when she gets back and what she does. And," he added, "keep a close eye on the boy. She's promised not to run, but I can't be certain she'll keep her word."

"Right, boss," Howard replied.

Jessie had planned to find a motel room for the night, but she was too anxious to sleep. Instead she kept driving. She had trusted Brant Mallery once and been badly hurt. She wasn't ready to do that again.

Self-loathing filled her as she recalled how strongly she had been attracted to John Adams. How could she be so stupid as to fall for Brant Mallery twice in one lifetime?

Her loathing shifted to him. He had no right to come barging into her life and lay claim to her son! Granted, he had been instrumental in producing Joey, but in her book, that didn't make him the father Joey deserved. She drew a shaky breath. What was she going to do?

No answer came. The only thing she was certain of was that she wanted to get back to Joey as quickly as possible. Stopping only for gas, she drove straight home.

Late in the night, Brant's phone rang. Waking from a restless sleep, he answered it. It was Howard Green. When Brant hung up, he was scowling. Jessie had driven directly back to the inn. She should have stopped and slept at some motel. She could have fallen asleep at the wheel. Suddenly a worried look replaced his anger. Tossing off his covers, he placed a call to the airport.

Chapter Five

Jessie frowned into her coffee cup. She hadn't slept well. Nightmares had plagued her. In one dream Brant had taken Joey away, and she had searched and searched and not been able to find them. She'd woken up in a sweat and rushed into Joey's room to make certain he was there.

For the rest of the night she had tossed and turned. At seven she had called Philip and asked him to stop by for breakfast before he went into his office. She had wanted some solid legal advice, but she didn't like what she was hearing.

"I know you're upset," Philip was saying in the same calm tones he used with a difficult client. "But what has happened is for the best. Joey was going to have to know about his real father sooner or later. And Brant Mallery should be helping pay for the boy's upbringing. It's expensive raising a child in this day and age.''

"I don't want any money from him," Jessie insisted through clenched teeth.

"You're not being reasonable," Philip scolded. "Brant Mallery is a wealthy man. He can give Joey advantages you can't. You don't want to deprive your son, do you?"

Jessie looked up from her coffee to glare at him. "It's the disadvantage of having Brant in our lives that worries me."

Reaching across the table, Philip took her hand in his. "Whether you like it or not, Brant Mallery does have a legal right to spend time with his son."

Jessie knew that was true, but she was scared. "I can retain full custody of Joey, can't I?" she asked anxiously. "He'll just have visiting privileges."

"It depends on the judge who hears the case and what demands Mallery makes. It isn't as though he actually deserted you and Joey. Your not telling him about his son could swing sympathy his way," Philip cautioned. "Did he give you any idea of what conditions he would be seeking?"

Jessie returned her attention to her coffee. "No."

Philip squeezed her hand. "Don't you worry. I'm going to do everything I can to protect you and

Joey.'' With his free hand, he caught her chin in his fingers and tilted her face upward. "Of course you might have an even better chance against Mallery if you showed up in court married to a prominent citizen—such as myself. We're comfortable together, Jessica. We could have a good marriage."

For Joey's sake, Jessie was tempted to accept. But the thought of sharing Philip's bed left her cold. She forced a smile. "I appreciate the offer, but I'm too upset to make a major decision like that at the moment."

"I just wanted you to know the door is open," Philip replied, leaning over to drop a light kiss on her lips.

Jessie tried to feel at least a small spark, but there was nothing. A sudden prickling at the back of her neck caused her to stiffen. She pulled free of Philip's light touch and turned around. Brant Mallery was watching them from the doorway.

Brant had entered the dining room in time to see Philip kiss Jessie. The action caused a cold anger to spread through him. The man wasn't right for her. He would stop this before it went any further. Crossing the room in long strides, he came to a halt beside the table. "I'd like to speak to Jess alone," he requested brusquely.

"I'm representing her," Philip replied, rising to

face Brant. "Anything you have to say to her will be said in front of me."

"This is a personal matter," Brant growled.

Jessie glanced around the dining room. Several of her guests were casting covert glances in the direction of her table. She didn't want them upset nor did she want her private life to become public gossip. She'd been through that kind of hell already. "It's all right, Philip," she interjected. Rising also, she added, "I'll speak to him alone. Mr. Mallery, will you follow me please?"

As she led Brant out of the dining room and toward her office, Philip followed.

"She said she'd speak to me *alone*," Brant told the lawyer coldly when he accompanied them into the office.

"I'm her lawyer and I'm advising her against doing that," Philip replied, moving past Brant to stand beside Jessie.

Brant's eyes narrowed threateningly on the lawyer. "Jess has no reason to be afraid of me."

"Considering your past actions, I have no reason to trust you," Philip countered.

"And I don't have time for this argument," Jessie snapped. "I have work to do. I can't expect Haddie and Melody to cook, serve and watch Joey by themselves forever."

"That's easily taken care of." Turning on his heel,

Brant strode out of the office. He'd wondered where Joey was. Now that he knew, he couldn't stop himself from going to find the boy.

Jessie started after him. Hearing footsteps behind her, she glanced over her shoulder to find Philip coming, too. "Wait here, please," she requested curtly. "We're beginning to look like a parade."

Philip frowned, obviously disgruntled, but did as she asked.

Reaching the kitchen, Jessie discovered Haddie standing by the stove holding a large skillet aimed threateningly at Brant. The normally calm and grandmotherly demeanor of the gray-haired, slightly plump cook was gone. In its place was a female warrior ready to do battle. Melody, the girl Jessie had hired to clean rooms and double as a waitress during meals, was standing behind Haddie, looking indecisive about what she should do with the two plates of scrambled eggs and ham she was holding. Jessie guessed that Brant was in danger of having them thrown at him. He was standing beside Joey's high chair watching the irate cook with a disconcerted expression on his face. "You get away from that child," Haddie was saying menacingly.

"It's all right," Jessie said. "I told you, Mr. Adams is really Brant Mallery."

"I remember," the cook replied, lowering the skillet but not putting it down entirely. "I just figured you wouldn't want him near Joey."

"I don't," Jessie admitted, "but I don't have much choice."

Brant's jaw tensed with anger. He knew he deserved Jessie's hatred but he didn't like it. Turning toward the boy, his expression softened. "Morning, big guy."

Joey who had been watching the proceedings with more interest than fear, smiled back. "Man play?"

Joey's growing attachment to "Mr. Adams" hadn't bothered Jessie. Now she felt torn. A part of her wished she hadn't allowed their friendship to develop. Another part of her knew it was healthy for Joey to have a good relationship with his father. She just wished she could trust Brant to be a good father.

"You, and your mom and I are going to have a little family discussion," Brant explained, extracting the boy from his chair.

"Play," Joey said again with a wide grin as Brant carried him out of the kitchen.

Still holding the skillet, Haddie frowned at Brant's departing back. "You just yell if you need any help," she told Jessie. "Melody and I will be there on the double."

"We sure will," Melody echoed, with a sharp nod of her head.

"Thanks," Jessie replied as she hurried after Joey and Brant.

Philip was waiting in the reception area, but this time he did not follow Brant back into Jessie's office. Instead, he stopped Jessie before she could enter and said worriedly, "I've got to be in court shortly."

Jessie was glad. She knew Brant Mallery well enough to know that if he wanted to talk to her alone, he was going to persist until he had. At least she wouldn't have to referee a battle between him and Philip.

"But I don't like leaving you here alone with Mallery," Philip was saying.

"I can handle myself," she assured him. "I'm not the naive girl I was when I first met him."

The frown on Philip's face deepened. "Don't sign anything. Don't even agree to anything verbally. Don't say anything to him if you can avoid it. I'll be back as soon as possible."

"Please, don't worry. I can handle this," she assured him again. She just wished she was as certain as she sounded.

Looking past her, Philip saw Brant watching them. As if staking his claim, Philip placed a second light kiss on Jessie's lips before saying goodbye.

A cold anger again filled Brant. "That's precisely what I came here to stop," he informed Joey in a low whisper.

The boy gave an answering gurgle.

"I knew you'd be on my side," Brant replied with a conspiratorial smile.

Entering the office, Jessie closed the door, then stood facing her nemesis. "I thought you weren't going to show up until the weekend." She wanted to snatch Joey from his arms, but she was determined not to act rashly.

"I was afraid you'd do something like that," he replied, his gaze passing her to rest coldly on the door as if he could see through it.

"Do what?" she demanded.

Joey looked anxiously from the man holding him to his mother. "Mommy," he said, holding out his arms to her.

Brant berated himself as he relinquished the boy to Jessie. He shouldn't have let his anger show. He'd frightened Joey and he'd made what he'd come to do more difficult. But it had galled him to see Philip kissing Jess as if she was his property. She deserved better than that pompous lawyer. He schooled his voice into a more moderate tone. "Running into Philip's arms isn't going to make this situation any easier."

"I didn't run into Philip's arms," Jessie informed him haughtily. "I merely thought it would be prudent to talk to a lawyer."

"Lawyers don't usually kiss their clients," Brant pointed out icily.

Jessie said nothing. She simply glared at him.

"You don't need protection from me, Jess." Turning away from her, he paced across the room. *Get yourself under control,* he ordered himself. *You're scaring Joey and making Jess angrier.* He returned to stand in front of her. In milder tones he said, "I know finding out that John Adams was me was a shock to you. I came here because I was afraid you might do something rash like marry Philip because you thought it would help you keep Joey away from me."

Jessie's back stiffened. It irritated her that he had guessed this was a ploy she might consider.

Brant saw her body straighten and knew he had been right. He raked an agitated hand through his hair. "I know you don't think I deserve to be a part of my son's life. I can only say that where you and I were concerned, I did what I thought was best for both of us. But I won't give up Joey."

Jessie's hold on her son tightened possessively, and Joey pressed his head into her shoulder as if he was frightened and needed to be closer to her for comfort.

Damn! Brant cursed mentally. He was already alienating his son. He drew a tired breath. "I'll make you a deal, Jess. I want a chance to prove to you that

I only want to share Joey's life, not take him away from you. You don't marry Reynolds for six months. You don't even get engaged to him. You give me time to get to know my son and let him get to know me and my family——his family. You let me set up a trust fund for him and help with his expenses. In return, I won't file for joint custody. When the six months are over, I'll leave it up to you to decide how often I get to see him." Brant knew he was taking a big chance. Jessie had to be harboring a great deal of anger and resentment toward him. But the woman he had known had a strong streak of fairness in her.

Jessie had to admit it sounded appealing. She only had to put up with him for six months and then she could banish him from her life, if she chose. But she was not ready to trust him so quickly. "How do I know you'll keep your word?"

Walking over to her desk, Brant found a clean sheet of paper. While she watched, he wrote out his conditions and his promise to not take her to court if she met those conditions. When it was completed, he signed it and handed it to her to read.

It was the bargain he had outlined. If she went to court she would be gambling with her and Joey's future. At least this way, after six months, she would have complete control once again. "You've got a deal," she said. Picking up a pen, she scrawled her name beneath his.

Brant drew a relieved breath. "Now will you tell Joey that I'm not the big bad monster?"

Jessie kissed the little cheek nestled into her shoulder. "It's all right, Joey," she said gently. "Mr. Mallery is a friend."

Brant frowned. "I think you should tell him I'm his father. That way he won't be confused when my mother refers to herself as his grandmother and my sister introduces herself as Aunt Carol."

Jessie felt her stomach knot. She knew that once she made this admission to Joey there would be no turning back. But it was too late to turn back now, anyway. "Mr. Mallery is your father...your daddy."

Joey lifted his head to look dubiously at Brant, then quickly reburied it in Jessie's shoulder.

Jessie read the disappointment on Brant's face and realized the powerful position she held. If she wanted, she could use Joey to hurt him as badly as he had hurt her. Their gazes met, and she saw in his eyes that he, too, knew she had this power. He raised a cynical eyebrow as if to ask if she planned to use it.

Jessie lowered her gaze to the child in her arms. She loved him too much to ever use him as a weapon for revenge. "Joey," she said cajolingly, "Mr. Mallery...Brant and I were just having a little argument. I have arguments with Haddie and we're all still friends.'' Joey lifted his head again but still didn't look convinced.

''I would like to be your friend, Joey,'' Brant said gently. He took a step toward Jessie but stopped when Joey again buried his head in Jessie's shoulder. Watching the mother and child, he had never felt so helpless, not even when he was lying partially paralyzed in the hospital.

Jessie knew what she had to do. She just didn't want to do it. *You agreed to give him a chance to prove himself as a father,* she reminded herself. She looked coolly at Brant to let him know that what she was about to do was distasteful to her. Then, forcing a smile for Joey's sake, she approached the man. Holding Joey with one arm, she placed the other around Brant's waist. ''You see, Joey, Brant and I are still friends.''

Brant put his arms loosely around the mother and child. It took every ounce of willpower he had not to crush them to him. He told himself he'd made the right decision when he'd asked Jessie for the divorce. He just wished she didn't feel so good in his arms. *Concentrate on the boy,* he ordered himself.

Standing in the circle of Brant's arms, Jessie wished she had thought of some other ploy. She had expected to feel disgust at his touch. Instead her knees felt weak and her heart was pounding erratically. A cold, self-directed anger filled her. How could she still harbor an attraction toward a man who had hurt her so badly? It was a mere instant of insanity that would never happen again, she assured herself. Releasing her hold on Brant, she slowly eased out of his arms.

The ploy had worked. Joey was smiling up at the man.

Brant glanced at Jessie to thank her and saw the coldness in her eyes. Clearly there was no love left for him in her heart. Probably for the best, he told himself, and turned his full attention to the boy. "I brought you a present."

"Just *one*, I hope," Jessie said, a note of caution in her voice. She wasn't going to let Brant spoil their son or try to buy his love.

"Just one." A crooked smile tilted one corner of his mouth. "I admit the temptation to buy out the entire store was strong. But I figured you wouldn't approve."

The momentary flash of mischief in his eyes when he admitted he had been tempted caused a peculiar warmth in her abdomen. Damn, the man was charming. But she'd fallen for that charm once and she wouldn't fall for it again. She stood Joey on the floor. "Why don't you go with your father and get your gift," she suggested with forced cheerfulness.

"It's in the lobby with my suitcase," Brant said, holding out his hand to the boy.

Joey gave Jessie one quick glance to assure himself that it was okay then, smiling happily, took the man's hand.

Left alone in the office, Jessie drew a deep breath. These reactions she was having to Brant Mallery were crazy. He was a cad. Granted he had married her and he had offered alimony. Yet he hadn't loved her, and that was what hurt, because she had loved him. "But I don't love him now and I will never love him again," she growled through clenched teeth.

Feeling as if she again had control of her emotions, she went out into the lobby. Brightly colored paper and ribbon was scattered on the floor around Joey. He was now trying to open the box that had been inside the wrapping. Brant squatted in front of the boy, helping. They eventually extracted a children's tape player, along with several tapes. "Let's clean this mess up and I'll show you how to use it," Brant said, beginning to gather the paper and ribbon while Joey examined his new toy.

"I'll clean it up," Jessie volunteered, her gaze resting on Brant's luggage.

Following the line of her vision, he said gruffly, "It's already Thursday. It would be foolish of me to return to Boston and then come back tomorrow. Do you have a room for me, or am I going to have to pay one of your guests to find other lodgings?"

He was a man who knew how to get his way, she thought dryly. Except where she and Joey were concerned, she amended firmly. This time he wasn't dealing with a starry-eyed, naive girl. This time she would prove to be a match for him. "I do have a room." It was the room she had reserved for John Adams. She'd kept it open an extra night, hoping he might return sooner than expected. Stupid fool! she berated herself. She still couldn't believe she had been ready to fall for Brant Mallery twice in one lifetime.

After giving Brant his key and making certain he and Joey were comfortably settled in the lounge, Jessie went back to the kitchen.

"Mr. Mallery will be staying and spending some time with Joey," she informed Haddie.

"Well, I just hope he doesn't get bored with the boy and leave him high and dry like he did you," the cook replied angrily.

"If he does, Joey will have you and me to make him feel loved. He'll forget about Brant Mallery quickly enough," Jessie replied. But as she poured herself a cup of coffee, renewed self-directed anger washed over her as she recalled her body's reaction to the feel of Brant's arms around her a few minutes earlier. Why couldn't she have found someone to love, someone who could hold her and vanquish these irrational reactions? *I've taken care of myself for years,* she told herself curtly. *I don't need anyone else's strength to see me through this.*

A knock on the kitchen door was followed by the entrance of Brant, carrying Joey.

"See." Joey proudly held out his new toy toward Haddie for her inspection. "Daddy give."

Haddie rewarded Brant with a cold glance. "You hurt either Joey or Jessie and this time you'll have *me* to answer to," she said threateningly.

"Haddie," Jessie interjected sharply, "I've made a deal with Mr. Mallery...Brant. It requires all of our cooperation."

Haddie was still scowling at the dark-haired man. "I'm not so certain it was a smart thing to do." Her gaze challenging, she asked Brant, "You planning to try to buy the boy's love with new toys? Sounds like the kind of shallow trick you might pull."

"I considered it," Brant admitted, "but Jess has already warned me not to try."

Haddie looked a little taken aback by this confession. Clearly she hadn't expected him to be so honest. "You just be careful what you do around here," she warned again.

Joey was again looking worried and Jessie didn't want to have to repeat the hugging. She wanted to keep as much distance between herself and Brant Mallery as possible. "Haddie, please," she pleaded in lowered tones. "Tell Joey you like his new toy."

Haddie glanced toward her and shook her head as if questioning Jessie's sanity. But when she returned her attention to the man and the boy, there was a forced smile on her face. "Right interesting thing you have there, Joey," she said. "What's it do?"

The smile returned to the child's face, and he pushed a button. A tune began to play.

Brant regarded the cook dubiously. "I was wondering if I could get some breakfast."

Haddie glared at him. "There's a diner in town. I hear all the truckers stop there."

"Haddie!" Jessie snapped. Turning to Brant, she said, "Take Joey out into the dining room. I'll see that you get your breakfast. What would you like?"

"Eggs and bacon," he replied, easing out of the kitchen. He succeeded in business by knowing when to retreat and when to stand his ground. This was definitely a time to retreat.

Alone with the cook, Jessie said tightly, "The deal I made with Brant will be null and void if we all don't cooperate. If you want him out of here in six months, you're going to have to be more hospitable."

"That six months is going to seem like six years," Haddie groused. "Never have liked being around a snake in the grass."

It'll seem more like six centuries to me, Jessie thought to herself. Aloud she said, "I want to take

Joey upstairs and change him out of his pajamas into his day clothes. Will you please fix Brant his breakfast?''

"Sure thing," Haddie replied, slamming a skillet on the stove.

Jessie glanced worriedly at the cook. When Haddie got that look in her eyes, Jessie was never certain what she would do. "You know that Joey's future is partially in your hands," she warned.

"I'll make Mr. Brant Mallery as welcome as he deserves to be," Haddie replied. "You just go ahead and take care of Joey."

"I want your promise that you'll do nothing but cook his breakfast and have Melody serve it to him," Jessie demanded.

"You have my word," Haddie replied, turning on the heat under the skillet.

Jessie gave the cook a final anxious glance as she left the kitchen. Taking Joey from Brant, she hurried upstairs and changed the boy as quickly as possible. "But not quickly enough," she muttered as she returned to the dining room.

The plate in front of Brant held burned toast, brown eggs and black bacon. But what amazed Jessie was that he was actually attempting to eat it. Haddie was watching from the doorway of the kitchen, and the look on her face told Jessie that her cook, too, was surprised.

"He must be real hungry," Melody said with wonder as she came to stand beside Jessie. "Do you think he'll get sick?" she asked in a worried whisper, watching him take a bite of the brown egg.

The thought that he might get sick shook Jessie. She told herself this was only because she had no desire to be put in the position of nursing him. She was still distressed by her body's reaction to the feel of his arms around her. "If he does, you and Haddie are going to take care of him," she snapped. Approaching the table, she said stiffly. "You hold Joey. I'll fix you a decent meal." Before he could respond, she had handed him their son and taken his plate.

"I told you to serve him a decent meal," she growled at the cook as she brushed past her and entered the kitchen.

"I didn't think he'd eat it," Haddie replied. Looking sheepish, she added, "I'll go get his orange juice and pour him a fresh glass."

Jessie scowled at her. "What did you do to the orange juice?"

"Just gave it a little salt for added flavor," the cook replied.

As she began to fix Brant a more palatable breakfast, Jessie wished he had thrown a fit. It would be more in keeping with the image she was determined to maintain of him. Then she reminded herself that he had gone so far as to marry her to get her into his

bed. He was a man who would do what he had to in
order to achieve his ends, she mused acidly, even if
it meant eating charcoal-broiled eggs.

When she returned to the dining room with the
new plate of food, she was surprised to find Howard
Green seated at the table with Brant. Mr. Green was
near Haddie's age, Jessie guessed. He was almost
bald. His hair, what was left of it, was white. He was
a large man, at least six foot two, and weighed
around two hundred pounds. But it appeared to be a
well-toned two hundred pounds.

"Jessie, will you join us?" Brant requested.
"There is one other condition to our deal that I didn't
mention earlier."

She didn't like being impolite in front of a guest,
but she'd had enough of his conditions. "We both
signed the agreement. There will be no more conditions. I have work to do. If you'll just hand over
Joey, I'll leave you to eat your breakfast in peace."

"Jess, we need to straighten this out right now,"
Brant insisted.

Haddie had been watching from the kitchen door.
Now she moved toward the table to stand protectively by Jessie's side.

Glancing around the room, Jessie was glad all the
other diners had eaten and gone. She braced herself.
She'd thought his deal had been too fair to be true.

Here comes the catch, she mused dryly. "What do we need to straighten out?"

"It concerns Joey and your safety," Brant replied. He nodded toward Mr. Green. "Howard is going to become your permanent bodyguard."

Jessie's eyes rounded in shock. "He's what?" In the next instant her shock turned to anger. "He's been working for you all along, hasn't he? He's been here spying on Joey and me ever since you left."

Haddie glared at Howard. "And here I was thinking what a nice man you were, helping me with my groceries, always coming into the kitchen to tell me how much you enjoyed my cooking. And all the time you were worming yourself into our lives just to get information."

"He wasn't spying," Brant insisted. "If he'd been spying I'd have known Jessie was coming to Boston."

"That just proves he isn't any good at his job," Haddie said haughtily.

With quiet dignity, Howard rose to face her. "I'm very good at my job, and my job was to make certain the boy and his mother were safe."

"They've always been safe enough before," Haddie replied, meeting his gaze coolly. "It wasn't until your boss came into the picture that they needed protection."

Ignoring the older couple, Jessie concentrated her

attention on Brant. "I don't need a bodyguard," she seethed. "And I resent this intrusion on my privacy."

Brant regarded her with an impatient scowl. "After the incident with Chase Murdock, you can't expect me to simply walk away and leave you and Joey unguarded."

"You walked away and left me once before," she reminded him curtly. She flushed when she realized what she had said. She had never meant to allow the depth of her hurt to show.

Brant's gaze became guarded. He had done what he had felt he had to do. "That was the past. This time I will not leave you unprotected."

Haddie looked at Jessie with concern. "What happened with Chase Murdock?"

"Nothing I couldn't have handled," Jessie replied, her back stiff with pride. The last thing she wanted from Brant Mallery was his protection.

"He got drunk and came up here when he thought she was alone," Brant elaborated, his gaze riveted on Jessie.

"Did he hurt you?" Haddie demanded. "'Cause if he did, he's going to answer to one of my skillets."

"No," Jessie assured her.

"Because I stopped him," Brant reminded her.

"I could have handled him," Jessie insisted, her

pride refusing to allow her to admit she had needed Brant Mallery's help.

"Maybe he's right about having a man around to protect you," Haddie said grudgingly. "There have been times when I've worried about one of your male guests trying to take advantage of you." Her gaze shifted to Brant. "Guess you'd know all about that."

Brant made no reply to Haddie's jab. Instead, he kept his attention on Jessie. "Howard is staying. You can consider him a permanent guest. I'll pay for his room by the year."

The set of his jaw told Jessie she was fighting a losing battle. "The first time I even get a hint he's acting as your spy, he's out," she warned.

"And," Brant continued, ignoring her warning, "I want you to call an electrician today. I want a buzzer hooked up to his room that will sound when you have a late arrival. I don't want you going down and answering the door by yourself in the middle of the night anymore."

"I resent you coming in here and taking over my life," Jessie fumed.

"I'm not taking over, I'm merely making a few adjustments for safety purposes," Brant replied in reasonable tones.

Jessie rewarded him with a scowl. "Is there anything else you want?"

You, a little voice in the back of his head answered. Curtly he pushed the thought away. Aloud, he said, "That should do for now."

"It had better do forever," Jessie stated, reaching for Joey.

"How about letting me entertain him while you work?" Brant suggested.

Already Jessie was beginning to worry about how much time Joey was spending with his father. She didn't want him to get too used to having Brant around. Past experience made her cautious about how long Brant would remain interested in his son.

"We'll stop by and see you at least once every half an hour," Brant bargained, reading the hesitancy in her eyes. "Remember, I can only be here on weekends. You'll have him the rest of the week."

Still not certain it was wise, Jessie nodded. Turning to Haddie, she said, "We need to work on the menus for the weekend."

"Should I expect my meals to be a bit on the overdone side from now on, too?" Howard asked the cook as she started toward the kitchen.

Haddie threw him a sharp glance. "As long as you remember you're a bodyguard and not a snitch, we'll get along just fine."

"Good-looking woman," Howard muttered with a smile as he reseated himself at Brant's table. "But I wouldn't want to cross her."

Brant glanced over his shoulder to make certain

the kitchen door was closed. Satisfied they were alone, he leaned close to Howard. "You're going to have to," he said in lowered tones. "I want you to find out all you can about Philip Reynolds. I also want to know how much time he spends with Jess."

"Is this where you tell me you've decided to remarry your ex and you want to know all you can about the competition?" Howard asked with a knowing smile.

Brant frowned into his coffee. "No," he said grimly. "It's over for me and Jess." Lifting his head, he again looked Howard in the eyes. "But Philip Reynolds isn't the right man for her, either. And I don't want to see her make another mistake." Glancing down at Joey, he said, "You don't want that pompous lawyer as a stepfather, do you?" When Joey looked up from his toy and smiled, Brant nodded approvingly at his son. "Didn't think so."

The smile on Howard's face was replaced by a worried look. "It's been my experience that women prefer to make their own mistakes where men are concerned. You could be buying trouble by interfering."

"Not if she doesn't find out," Brant replied. "I'm counting on your discretion."

Howard shook his head. "Guess I'd better enjoy my meals while I can. How'd that burned stuff taste anyway?"

"Like shoe leather," Brant replied. "So be careful."

In the kitchen, Jessie pulled out the menu and slammed it down on the counter. "That man is the most exasperating human being I have ever met. Can you believe him? He waltzes into my life and starts telling me how to live it."

"Well, I do have to admit I like the idea of your having a man around to protect you," Haddie said, casting her gaze briefly toward the closed door. "'Course I'll be certain to keep a close eye on Mr. Howard Green to make sure that bodyguarding is all he's doing."

Jessie, too, looked at the closed door. For the moment she'd go along with Brant's wishes. But this time he wasn't going to turn her world topsy-turvy.

Chapter Six

"You look very nice."

Jessie glanced up from changing Joey's diaper to find Brant leaning against the doorjamb. His expression was guarded and the level tone of his voice left her wondering if it was a real compliment, or if he was merely being polite. "Thanks," she replied coolly.

"You seem a little nervous," he observed, entering the room and joining her beside the crib.

Jessie breathed a worried sign as she fastened Joey's pajamas. "Philip isn't going to like the idea that I signed an agreement without consulting him first."

"So you've planned an intimate little dinner in

your office, complete with a table set with flowers and candles.'' He paused when she turned towards him with a questioning scowl. ''I peeked in on my way upstairs,'' he explained. ''Anyway, you've planned this little tête-à-tête to convince him you did the right thing.''

He made it sound as if she planned to seduce Philip in order to gain his approval. ''He's my lawyer and I want to have a private discussion with him,'' she replied curtly.

Brant's smile did not reach his eyes. ''Well, I've come to do my part,'' he said, picking up Joey and holding him over his head. The boy squealed with laughter and the smile on Brant's face became genuine.

Jessie again wondered if she was allowing the father and son too much time together. She had been planning to hire a local girl to baby-sit Joey tonight, but Brant had insisted on the job and she'd been too anxious about facing Philip to argue. ''He gets a little snack around seven and I try to get him into bed by eight,'' she instructed. ''If you have any problems, Haddie will help.''

Brant greeted this statement with a raised eyebrow.

''Your lunch was fine,'' Jessie pointed out, in answer to Brant's unspoken question. ''I've convinced her that this arrangement is best for all concerned, and she has agreed to cooperate.'' *I just hope I can convince Philip of the same thing,* she added to her-self.

"You go have a good time. Joey and I will be just fine," he assured her.

Watching the man and boy together, Jessie could see the bond forming between them. But she could not help worrying that Brant's side of the bond might be badly flawed, and eventually snap. She drew a shaky breath. She'd deal with that problem if and when it arose. Right now, she had to concentrate on Philip. After giving Joey a quick kiss, she hurried downstairs to check on her arrangements.

Brant waited until she was gone, then he turned to Joey and said, "I've been watching you and Philip together. You're not good pals. In fact, I've never seen him hold you or play with you. He is definitely not the right stepfather for you. Agreed?" He shook his head to emphasize his words.

Smiling brightly, Joey shook his head, too.

Brant nodded approvingly. "I thought so." According to their deal, Jessie was to wait six months before making a commitment to Philip, but Brant could not get the picture of the table in her office out of his mind. "I've had a lot of business dinners with my lawyers," he informed Joey. "But your mother's arrangements look more like the setting for a romantic rendezvous." Smiling thoughtfully, he kissed the tip of the child's nose. "We'll have to make certain they keep their meeting strictly business. Right?"

Joey made a jumble of pleased sounds.

"Glad we're in agreement," Brant replied with a satisfied laugh.

"I hope this means you've been considering my proposal and have decided to accept," Philip said as Jessie led him into her office.

Jessie had never been good at pretense, and she didn't believe in playing games with people. There were a dozen practical reasons, if she was to marry again, Philip would be an excellent choice. But she knew she was never going to accept his proposal. "I respect and admire you—" she began.

Philip held up his hand. "That does not sound like the beginning of an acceptance speech," he observed with a disappointed grimace. Glancing toward the table, he frowned. "Is this a 'Dear Philip' dinner?"

"Actually it's an 'I've done something that is probably going to make you angry but I want you to forgive me and still be my friend and my lawyer' dinner," she replied.

Turning back toward her, he gave her an encouraging smile. "I will always be your friend and lawyer."

It occurred to Jessie that after his initial show of disappointment, Philip didn't seem all that upset by her rejection of his marriage proposal. *I guess I'm just not the kind of woman who inspires undying passionate yearning in the men in my life,* she thought dryly. But in this case, it was just as well.

"Can I assume this has something to do with Mallery?" Philip asked, bringing her thoughts back to the purpose of the dinner.

Jessie crossed to her desk, picked up the agreement she'd signed with Brant and handed it to him. While he read it, she poured them each a glass of wine.

Finishing the document, Philip laid it back on the desk and faced her grimly. "As your lawyer, how many times have I told you never to sign anything without consulting me first?" he demanded sternly.

"Many," she replied, handing him his glass. "But it seemed like a reasonable deal. In six months, if I so choose, I can kick him out of my and Joey's life."

"He did agree to that," Philip confirmed. He placed a protective arm around Jessie's shoulders. "And I'll see that he keeps his part of the bargain."

Jessie smiled up at him gratefully. "Thanks."

A sudden knock on the door was followed immediately by Brant's entrance. Joey was with him, perched happily in the crook of his arm. Brant's gaze traveled coolly along Philip's arm, which was still around Jessie's shoulders. "I hope you two haven't decided to break our agreement."

"No," Philip replied, releasing his hold on Jessie as his manner became that of the excellent lawyer he was. "However, I would like to call in a couple of witnesses to countersign this agreement, just to make it a bit more official."

Brant drew a quiet breath of relief. But he wasn't finished. Now, he decided, was as good a time as any to observe the true extent of the friendship between Joey and Philip. "I'll get Haddie and Howard," he volunteered. "You hold Joey." He pushed the boy into Philip's arms. Immediately Joey looked unhappy. He stretched his arms out toward Brant, then toward Jessie, clearly willing to go to either of them but not pleased at staying where he was.

Philip looked as disconcerted as Joey. Obviously he had no idea what to do with Joey, and he showed no interest in making an attempt to placate the child. "You'd better take him, Jessica," he said, quickly handing the boy to her.

Jessie caught the glimmer of satisfaction in Brant's eyes as he strode out of the room, and her back stiffened with annoyance. She hadn't needed his little demonstration to show her that Philip and Joey weren't the best of pals. But they weren't enemies, either.

"Who's Howard?" Philip asked watching Brant's departing back.

"Brant has decided Joey and I need protection," Jessie answered. "Howard's our bodyguard."

Philip frowned musingly. "I hate to admit it, but he's right. There have been moments when I've worried about you running this place alone."

Jessie shook her head. "I've done fine all these years. Suddenly everyone thinks it's great that a strange man is going to be hovering around in the background watching Joey and me all of the time."

"Protecting Joey and you," Brant corrected, returning to the room with Haddie and Howard in tow.

"Where's the paper?" Haddie questioned briskly. "I've got food cooking on the stove."

"There." Philip motioned toward the desk with one hand while handing her a pen with the other. Then, turning his attention toward Brant, he said, "I expect your man to respect Jessica's privacy."

"I'll see to it that he does," Haddie said curtly, as she scribbled her name on the paper. Straightening, she extended the pen toward Howard. "I'm keeping my eyes on him, and the first inkling I get that he's passing information back to his boss about any of our movements, he'll be sorry he ever set foot in my kitchen." Tossing Howard a final warning glance, she stalked out of the room.

Watching her departing back, Howard smiled. "Fine figure of a woman," he muttered as he signed the paper. "Bit of a temper, though."

"And now that that's taken care of," Philip said as Howard laid the pen aside, "I would appreciate it if you two gentlemen, and I'm using that term loosely, would leave, so that Jessica and I can get on with our dinner." Taking Joey from Jessie, he handed him to Brant. "I believe you have your son for the evening."

"Don't you think I should stay and go over the details of the agreement with you? Just so we both understand all of the finer points," Brant suggested in businesslike tones.

"The terms are clearly spelled out," Philip assured him, adding with a tone of dismissal, "Good evening."

As the door closed, and Philip and Jessie were once again alone, the lawyer eyed Jessie speculatively. "It's clear to me that Mallery came in here to disrupt our evening. Just what are his intentions toward you? Is he trying to win you back?"

For one brief moment Jessie found herself wishing that he was. *Fool!* she chided herself. "He's not interested in me," she replied. "Obviously he's simply not ready for Joey to have a stepfather."

"Well, you let me know if he gives you any trouble," Philip instructed.

Trouble, Jessie thought, *should be Brant Mallery's middle name.* Looking at the table, she suddenly visualized him sharing a romantic dinner with her, and the blood rushed through her veins. Damn! After what he had done to her, how could she have a fantasy like that! Angrily pushing the man from her mind, she concentrated on Philip. "Tell me about your day in court," she encouraged.

Upstairs in Joey's room, Brant played with his son, but his mind was on the couple downstairs. "Well, we did what we could for the moment," he muttered and was rewarded by a flood of happy chatter from Joey.

He picked up the boy and gave him a hug. "I wish things could be different for the three of us—you, me and your mom," he said gruffly. "But they can't. I know she'll remarry one of these days. We just have to make certain she chooses the right man."

Wiggling free, Joey found his ball and tossed it at Brant. "Right man," he mimicked.

"Yes," Brant said stiffly. "We have to make certain she finds someone who will love her as much as you and—" He stopped before he added the "I." If she knew the whole truth she wouldn't want his love, anyway. "As much as you do," he finished.

Philip left around nine. Jessie went upstairs to check on Joey and found Brant rocking him. The child was sound asleep, and Brant looked well on his way to dozing.

"He didn't want to go to bed," Brant explained drowsily as Jessie lifted Joey from his arms.

"You're going to spoil him," she fussed in hushed tones. She carried the boy to his crib and laid him in it. He squirmed, and she gently patted his bottom until he settled back into a deep sleep.

"Every time I laid him down, he started to wake up and cry," Brant explained in a low whisper. "I didn't know about patting him. I'm new at this fatherhood business."

Jessie bit her tongue to keep herself from reminding him that was his fault not hers. "Good night," she said instead. "Please lock Joey's door on your way out."

Exiting through the adjoining bathroom, she went into her bedroom. She was reaching for the zipper of her dress when Brant's voice interrupted.

"You aren't seriously considering marrying Philip, are you?" he asked.

Whirling around, she discovered he had followed her. She had thought she had her emotions under control, but seeing him in her bedroom brought a rush of hurt and anger. "Get out of my room!" she ordered.

Ignoring her command, he closed the door between her room and the bathroom, then turned to face her again. "You didn't answer my question."

He didn't want her, so why should he care whom

she married? she raged. Aloud she said, "It's none
of your business."

His jaw tensed. A part of him said she was right,
and the fury in her eyes warned him that he was
treading on dangerous ground. But he couldn't get
the picture of her and Philip out of his mind. "It is
my business," he replied. "The man you marry will
be Joey's stepfather. He and that Reynolds character
don't even get along."

That she had already decided not to marry Philip
didn't matter. Brant had no right to interfere. "If I
were to marry Philip, he and Joey would get along
just fine," she snapped. "Philip is a little nervous
around small children, but he is a good, kind, decent
man who understands the meaning of the word commitment."

Brant flinched at the verbal blow. He deserved it.
Still, it irked him to hear her defending Philip so
vehemently. "You told me once you didn't love
Reynolds. Do you really want that kind of sterile
marriage? Do you think it will create the right kind
of environment for Joey to grow up in?"

Jessie trembled with fury. "First you abandon me
and then you come back and try to dictate how I
should lead my life." She pointed toward the door.
"Get out!"

"I never meant to abandon you," Brant defended.
"I told you what happened."

"Right," she seethed. "You were in an accident, and to save me from a life of self-sacrifice you kept the truth from me and demanded a divorce. Then you recovered. But the time in the hospital gave you a chance to reevaluate our relationship and you decided that whatever we had between us wasn't love and you were better off without it. What it boils down to is that you decided you wanted to go your way without me and left me to go my way. Well, I have, and you're not invited along for the ride."

Brant knew he should back off, but instead he heard himself saying, "I just don't want to see you making a mistake."

"A *second* mistake," she corrected acidly.

Suddenly worried that he might be pushing her into Philip's arms, Brant moved toward her. "You deserve to marry a man you love," he said gruffly. "You deserve to have a full, happy life." His hands closed around her upper arms. "Don't settle for less, Jess."

Heat rushed through her. How could she be so angry at him and still be so sensitive to his touch? "I tried that once. It didn't work," she replied. She'd meant the statement to be issued with biting sarcasm. But when she met his gaze, she suddenly found herself lost in the warm, pleading depths of his eyes. Her voice shook when she spoke, and her chin trembled.

"Jess." Brant whispered her name as the passion-darkened brown eyes that had haunted his dreams for so long gazed up at him.

She stood motionless, barely breathing. Tears of anger and frustration burned at the back of her eyes. How could she still desire him after all the pain he had caused her? Furious with herself, she tried to pull away.

Brant's hold on her tightened. "Jess," he said again, his voice a velvet caress. His mouth moved toward hers. His whole body ached to taste her, to touch her again. The vision of the two of them as lovers filled his mind. Suddenly the cold chill of reality washed over him. His body stiffened. He released his hold and moved away from her. He'd made the right decision in the hospital. If he gave in to this desire he was feeling, he would only hurt them both. Raking a hand agitatedly through his hair, he said gruffly, "Sorry."

A cold, hard lump formed in Jessie's abdomen as she watched his withdrawal. Obviously he found any lingering attraction he felt for her distasteful. The sharp pang of rejection was overwhelmed by self-directed anger mingled with humiliation. She had been ready to melt in his arms. Stupid! Stupid! Stupid! she ranted at herself. The tears at the back of her eyes burned even hotter. She had to get rid of him. "I have already told Philip I can't marry him," she confessed. "Now that that's settled, get out!"

Silently, Brant obeyed. He had been so certain he had his emotions under control. Striding down the hall to his own room, he promised himself he would never weaken like that again.

Alone in her room, Jessie stood with her hands balled into fists. "Damn," she cursed as the tears she had been holding back began to flow down her cheeks. She couldn't believe how willing she had been for him to kiss her. "It will never happen again," she promised herself.

The next morning Jessie's cool reserve was firmly back in place. Still she would have preferred to avoid any private conversations with Brant. That, however, was impossible. Joey's birthday was coming up in a few days. She had considered not mentioning this fact to Brant, but she had struck a bargain with him; not telling him about his son's birthday could invalidate their deal.

She put it off until midafternoon. Finally, when Joey was taking his afternoon nap, she forced herself to seek out Brant. He was outside, sitting on a bench built around the base of a large old oak. It was the same bench they had sat on during the days before and just after their marriage happily discussing their future. A future that was nothing but fantasy to him, she reminded herself curtly. Her chin trembled and she forced the memories from her mind. "I need to speak to you," she said stiffly, halting beside the bench.

Brant had been sitting with his eyes closed, old memories filling his mind. The sound of Jessie's voice startled him, and an uneasiness stirred within him. If it was possible to turn back the clock he would. "What is it?" he asked evenly.

Jessie's jaw twitched. Being in this spot with him provoked intense anger. She had cared so much and now it was clear he had cared very little. Shoving these thoughts from her mind, she said, "Joey's birthday is next Thursday. I just thought you might like to know." Unwilling to linger even a moment longer than necessary, she turned and walked swiftly back toward the inn.

Brant caught up with her on the porch. "Are you planning a party?"

"Just a small one with me and Haddie," she replied. As an afterthought she added, "I suppose we'll invite your Mr. Green. No sense in him having watch from the sidelines."

"I'd like to be here," Brant said.

Jessie had guessed he would want to, but she had hoped business would keep him away. He was not an easy man to ignore, and the amount of time he was spending at the inn was taking its toll on her nerves. Now she said with schooled nonchalance, "Of course you can come. It is part of our bargain."

Brant knew she didn't want him there, but he couldn't make himself stay away. "Thanks," he replied.

Several times during the next couple of days he found himself wondering if it was a mistake to force himself into Jess's life once again. Being near her was harder than he'd ever dreamed it would be.

"I'm doing what's best for all of us," he told himself sternly as he drove home at the end of the weekend. The problem was, it made him feel like hell.

Once Brant was gone, Jessie expected to experience a rush of relief. Instead, a sense of apprehension lingered. Sitting at her desk, she frowned skeptically as she reread the part of his agreement where he promised to get out of their lives if she requested he do so at the end of the six months. The frown on her face deepened. She wondered if he would really keep that part of the bargain. Grudgingly, she admitted that she didn't know Brant Mallery well enough to predict his actions. There was a time when she had thought she did, but not anymore. Her jaw tensed. Philip had said this document would be binding in a court of law.

Trying to put Brant out of her mind, she shoved

the agreement into the safe and went to look for Joey. She'd left him in the kitchen with Haddie.

"Joey's out back, watching Howard chop wood," Haddie informed her when Jessie found the cook alone in the kitchen. "Been watching them out the window. Joey's been sitting on the step, keeping well away from the ax and wood splinters," she added quickly as if worried that Jessie might think she was shirking her duty.

"I thought Peter was supposed to come by today and get our woodpile in order," Jessie said, joining Haddie to watch the man and boy outside.

"He's got a touch of the flu," Haddie replied. She wrinkled her brow. "Can't say I like having a spy around, but it is handy having a man to do a few chores."

Jessie glanced at the older woman. There was anger in Haddie's eyes, the kind caused by a sense of betrayal. Jessie recalled that during the preceding week, before Howard's true reason for being here had been exposed, he and the cook had seemed to develop a rather friendly relationship. Well, at least she found out the truth about him before she went and fell in love with him, Jessie thought philosophically as she started toward the back door.

Howard saw her when she stepped onto the back porch and, after burying the ax in the stump he had been using as a base for his wood chopping, he approached her. "You've got a fine son, Mrs. Mallery," he said sincerely.

When Brant had been a dark shadow from her past, Jessie hadn't minded being called Mrs. Mallery. But now that he had returned to her life, the name caused a twist of pain. "Please call me Jessie," she requested.

Extending his hand toward her, he smiled a friendly smile. "I'm Howard, and if there is anything I can do for you or Joey, you just tell me."

She was tempted to tell him that he could go away and tell Brant to stay away, too. But she held her tongue.

As if he could read her mind, Howard said gently, "Don't judge Brant too severely. He's a decent man. That accident should have killed him. It's a miracle he's alive. But it changed him. He keeps people more at a distance now." He glanced toward Joey. "Except for that little guy. He really cares for him."

He just doesn't care for Joey's mother, Jessie thought acidly, then berated herself. She had to put the past behind her. Brant had touched death. In spite of the hurt he had inflicted on her, she was glad he had not died, and she couldn't blame him for reevaluating his life. Besides, she concluded, it was better to have found out early that his love for her wasn't genuine. She would not have wanted to remain in a marriage where the love was only one-sided. She would have been hurt in the end, anyway. This way it was over quickly. As if to call her a liar, her stomach twisted painfully and she suddenly found herself remembering the excited expectation she had felt when she thought he was going to kiss her. *It's over!* she told herself. Aloud, she said, "I'll be interested in seeing how long his caring lasts this time."

The moment the words were out, she regretted them. She didn't want anyone to guess how deep her hurt still was. She didn't even want to admit it to herself. Damn! she cursed mentally. Her jaw taut with pride, she picked up Joey and stalked back into the house.

Brant arrived midmorning on Joey's birthday. Standing at her office window, Jessie watched him walk from the parking area. This time she was prepared for him. This time he would not get past her defenses. This time she would maintain a cool, dignified demeanor around him at all times.

She noted that he was carrying a single large box. At least he hadn't gone overboard on presents. Unless he has a trunkful he couldn't carry, she amended. If that was the case, he was going back to Boston with them. Her son wasn't for sale, and she wasn't going to allow Brant to try to buy him.

Walking out to the reception desk, she greeted Brant politely and gave him his room key. As usual he refused to allow her to carry his suitcase to his room. But he did give her the gift for Joey. "Just put it with the others," he said.

"So far so good," she muttered, adding his package to the others hidden in her office closet. Joey was in the kitchen with Haddie "helping" to bake his birthday cake. Jessie guessed Howard was in there, too. The man did seem to show a marked interest in her cook. "It's just a shame he has to work for someone like Brant Mallery," she mused aloud, closing the closet door.

"I can't blame you for having a low opinion of me..."

Jessie whirled around. Brant was standing in the doorway of her office, his expression grim. Her defenses went up.

"...but I did what I thought was for your good, as well as mine," he finished.

"You're right," she conceded. "I wouldn't want a husband who didn't want me."

Brant's body went rigid as he fought for control. *Not want her.* How he wished that was the truth. Reaching into his pocket, he pulled out a small, elegantly wrapped gift. "This is for you," he said, extending it toward her.

Jessie took a step back. She didn't want anything from him. "There's no reason for you to give me a gift," she said, refusing to accept the package.

"It's a small token of my gratitude," he replied insistently, "for bearing my son."

Jessie's lip trembled. The picture of her hospital room filled her mind. In the bed next to hers was another new mother. The baby's father came in, his face flushed with pleasure. "Thank you," he had said with loving tenderness to his wife, who lay holding their new daughter. A lump of anger formed in Jessie's throat. She had given birth to Joey alone, with no loving husband to share her pain and her joy. "I didn't do it for you," she said in a low growl. Hot tears burned at the back of her eyes as the desertion she'd felt when she'd received his demand for a divorce washed over her. She had to get away from him now, before she said something she might regret. Moving with stiff formality, she headed for the door.

But as she moved past him, Brant stopped her, his steel grasp closing around her arm, forcing her to remain. "I know how much you must hate me," he said gruffly. "But I never meant to hurt you."

Hate him. That was what she wished she could do. Life would be much easier. She had thought she did hate him. But hate wouldn't make her blood race the way it did when he touched her. "Let go of me!" she snarled, more angry with herself than him.

Ignoring her demand, he maintained his firm grip on her arm. "This belongs to you," he said without

compromise. With his free hand, he again extended
the package toward her.

"I want nothing from you," she ground out. *Only
your love,* the little voice in her head corrected. Her
mouth tightened against this thought and she struggled to pull free.

Brant had hoped for a truce, but where Jess was
concerned, nothing seemed to go right. Releasing her
abruptly, he strode to the desk. He placed the present
on the blotter and said grimly, "Don't think of this
as being from me. Think of it as being from Joey's
great-grandmother. She gave it to me to give to the
mother of my firstborn son. It's supposed to bring
luck and joy to the owner."

Jessie's shoulders straightened with pride. "I'm
sure she meant for you to give it to someone you
love," she said. That was all she had meant to say,
but before she could stop herself, she heard herself
adding dryly, "That is, if you are actually capable
of loving someone."

Capable of loving someone! His hands closed
around her upper arms and he lifted her toward him.
He wanted to kiss her so badly it was a physical pain.

Jessie saw his mouth moving toward hers. *Turn
away!* she ordered herself. But her body refused to
respond.

Don't be a fool! Brant's inner voice screamed at
him. *What happens after you kiss her? You can't let*

this go any further. His hands tightened painfully on her arms, then abruptly he released her. "It's yours," he growled. "You may do with it what you like. Throw it away if that pleases you." Without giving her a chance to respond, he strode out of the room.

Jessie stood frozen as the door slammed shut behind him. She wasn't certain what had happened except that she had embarrassed herself again. That his love for her hadn't lasted didn't mean he was incapable of loving. Vacation romances happened; she'd seen them happen to others. But even worse, when she thought he was going to kiss her, she'd been willing to allow it. At least he realized his feelings for her went no further than lust, and he was being strong enough not to give in to them this time. He wouldn't want to make a second *mistake,* she thought acidly.

Slowly she walked to her desk and sat down. The elegantly wrapped gift blurred in front of her. Frustration enveloped her as she realized her eyes were filling with tears. She leaned back in her chair and closed them. Two thin streams of salty water trickled down her cheeks. She had never cried over Brant before.

Following their brief honeymoon, she had been anxious and worried after he'd left and hadn't called her as promised. When she'd tried to call him and he didn't return her call she had been confused and

hurt. Still she had not cried. She had never been one
to cry without knowing what she was crying about.
Then his letter asking for a divorce had arrived. She
had known something was wrong, but the contents
of the letter had been a shock. She'd felt as if she'd
been punched in the stomach. But her pride had refused to allow her to cry. Now, after all these years,
the unshed tears demanded to be released. "Every
girl deserves to have at least one good cry over a
broken romance," she murmured as she gave up the
struggle for control and allowed the rivers of salty
water to pour down her cheeks.

Not wanting to be heard, she made almost no
sound as deep, soul-wrenching sobs shook her. Beginning to feel sick, she wanted to go to her room,
but she couldn't pass through the lobby with her eyes
red and swollen and her face wet with tears. Enough!
she told herself, taking deep breaths to quell the nau-
sea. Slowly the crying subsided and she dried her
face. As her eyes focused on the gift still sitting in
the middle of the desk blotter, her jaw tensed. For a
moment, she was tempted to throw it in the trash,
but Brant had said it had come from his grandmother.
She couldn't treat a family heirloom in so cavalier a
fashion. Opening her safe, she placed the still-
wrapped package in the farthest, darkest corner.
Closing the heavy door, she wished she could place
Brant in the farthest, darkest corner of her mind and

shut him out of her life behind a heavy steel door. Maybe at the end of six months she could, she told herself hopefully. But if his feelings toward Joey proved sincere, she knew she wouldn't. "I'll deal with that when the time comes," she muttered.

As she drew a tired breath, she pulled out her books. Doing a little accounting would give her eyes and face time to clear away the evidence of her tears. And she need not worry about relieving Haddie and Howard of the duty of watching Joey. She was certain Brant would have already done that.

An hour later, she was totaling the figures on the final page of the ledger, when she was interrupted by a knock, followed by Brant's entrance. To her surprise he didn't have Joey with him. He closed the door and moved toward the desk. "I've just received a call from my secretary," he said. "I had planned to stay through the weekend, but an urgent business matter has arisen, one I have to handle personally. I'll have to leave early tomorrow."

Jessie knew it would be impolite to shout "hurrah!" but she could not help breathing a sigh of relief. It was obvious she needed more time to work on her control where Brant was concerned. She saw him scowl. Well, the fact she didn't want him here couldn't have come as a surprise, she thought dryly. As he reached the desk, she noticed him glance toward the trash basket behind it and the scowl on his face deepen.

She opened the safe and withdrew the gift. "You keep it," she said with terse command, adding, "if you're still around when Joey gets married, you can give it to him to give to his wife."

For a moment Brant looked as if he planned to argue with her. Then with a scowl of resignation, he took the gift and shoved it into his pocket. "I was planning to wait for a better time," he said levelly. "But since I'll be leaving early tomorrow, I'll have to make my request now."

A prickling sensation traveled up Jessie's back. Every instinct told her she wasn't going to like this request.

"Thanksgiving is coming up in a couple of weeks," he continued in the same level tones. "I would like for you and Joey to come to Boston and spend it with me and my family. My mother and sister are anxious to meet both of you."

Jessie wanted to say no. She'd figured that his mother and sister would want to meet Joey; after all, he was Brant's son. But she guessed they would probably prefer that she not exist. She knew that Brant was a member of the higher social circles in Boston and suspected that one of his reasons for wanting to dissolve their marriage had been his re-alization that she would not fit in with his family and friends. Momentarily she considered saying that she couldn't ask Haddie to take over the inn for such an important holiday. But that wasn't true. Haddie could handle everything just fine. Besides, this meeting was inevitable and she might as well get it over with. "Fine," she agreed. "We'll be there."

"I'll send you plane tickets and meet you at the airport," he said in brisk tones. "I was thinking you could fly in on Wednesday and stay until Sunday."

Five days with people who didn't want her around? This time Jessie balked. "I really can't be away from the inn for that long during a holiday weekend," she lied. "Wednesday to Friday is going to have to do."

"Wednesday to Friday it is then," he replied. "I'll make the arrangements now."

Jessie noted that he hadn't seemed all that disappointed by her insistence on shortening the visit. And as he left, she sensed an uneasiness about him. It wasn't obvious, but it was there, just a tiny shadow peeking out. Clearly, he was as anxious about her meeting his family as she was about meeting them. More than ever she was convinced they would not approve of her. "But I have to face them sooner or later. No point in putting off the inevitable," she told herself grimly.

Chapter Seven

No amount of preparation could have readied Jessie for her first sight of Brant's home, a country estate outside Boston. When he turned the Mercedes onto the long, tree-lined drive, she tensed. She had expected a large home, but at the sight of the huge, three-story brick manor house, three times the size of her inn, her courage threatened to fail her. A perfectly manicured lawn accented with gardens and shrubs gave the place a daunting formal appearance. Brant was right, she thought frantically. She didn't belong here. Then she stiffened with pride. Wealth didn't make these people better than her. She was as good as any of them.

Still, as she climbed out of the car and followed

Brant across the wide stone drive to the marble steps leading to the front door, her legs felt shaky. She wished she had Joey to clutch for moral support, but Brant was carrying him.

And Brant hadn't made this any easier for her, she fumed. His manner had been guarded ever since he had met her and Joey at the airport, and the uneasiness she had sensed in him the day he'd issued the invitation was even stronger.

Suddenly the front door opened and a pretty young woman in her early twenties, with dark hair and eyes that matched Brant's and Joey's, came rushing out. She was expensively dressed in designer jeans and a sweater that hadn't come off a department-store rack. But her voice and face were open with welcome as she shrieked, "You're here at last! We've been waiting on pins and needles."

Behind her, coming at a slower pace, was an older woman, in her early fifties, whom Jessie guessed must be Brant's mother. Her once dark hair, which was now streaked with gray, was carefully arranged in a sophisticated style. Unlike her daughter, she was dressed more formally in a lightweight wool suit. The teal color of her outfit accentuated the creaminess of her still youthful-looking skin and pretty, delicately featured face. Like her daughter, her smile of welcome seemed open and genuine.

Their greeting is for Joey, not me, Jessie reminded

herself cynically as both women gave Brant and Joey their full attention. But the thought was barely finished before they turned to her.

"Jessie." The older woman smiled kindly and, taking Jessie's hand in hers, gave it a friendly squeeze. "We're so glad you've come."

The younger woman gave Jessie a confirming smile, then turned toward Brant and scowled impatiently at him. "My brother keeps secrets he shouldn't," she said. Her smile reappeared as she turned her attention back to Jessie. "Welcome," she said sincerely.

Stunned by the friendly reception, Jessie managed a quiet "Thank you."

"If you haven't already guessed," Brant interjected, before his mother and sister took complete control. "Jess, this is my mother, Doris, and my sister, Carol."

"I'm pleased to meet you, Mrs. Mallery," Jessie said, wondering if this was real. She had been so certain she would be received coldly. "And Carol."

"It's Doris," Mrs. Mallery corrected with an encouraging smile. "Come on inside. I've ordered coffee brought to the living room." A note of apology entered her voice. "I hope you don't mind, but Carol and I couldn't resist buying a few things for Joey. We'll try not to spoil him, but just this once, I'm afraid we went a little overboard."

Overboard was a good description, Jessie thought as they entered the large room to find a pyramid of prettily wrapped boxes.

"I'm sorry, Jess," Brant apologized. "I told them to control themselves."

"Actually we did," Carol interjected. "I wanted to buy one of everything in the shop." Suddenly turning to Jessie, she gave her a tight hug. "I'm so excited about being an aunt."

To Jessie's surprise, Brant's mother followed her daughter's cue and gave Jessie a hug, too. "Thank you," she said. Then she looked at Joey, and tears filled her eyes. "He looks just like Brant at that age."

Jessie caught the very slight twitch of Brant's jaw. So his new look did bother him. She wanted to tell him that it shouldn't. He might not be as handsome as he once was, but he was still a very masculine and attractive man. But that, she decided, would not be a good idea. Besides, he wouldn't be interested in hearing that from her.

"I hope you don't mind," Doris said, breaking into Jessie's thoughts. "Brant wanted his old nursery in the west wing fixed up for Joey. And since I assumed you would want your room next to Joey's, I had the governess's room cleaned and prepared for you. It opens directly onto the nursery and shares a bath with it."

"That sounds very nice," Jessie assured her.

But Doris continued to frown worriedly. She glanced at her son, and her jaw hardened as if she was making a decision. "The west wing is Brant's domain. Carol and I have rooms in the east wing. If you would feel more comfortable, we can easily shift everything to more neutral ground."

Jessie saw Carol watching her anxiously. Clearly the mother and daughter were under the impression that she and Brant were not on friendly terms. Well, they weren't. But they had a truce of sorts for the next five months, and she was going to keep up her end. If Brant wanted Joey in his old nursery, she would not challenge him on this. "I'm sure the arrangements you have made will be just fine," she replied evenly.

Defiantly, Doris met the angry look on her son's face. "I felt it was only proper to offer." Her voice held a strong note of disapproval as she added, "It's not fair for you to make all the rules. People should be given a choice."

Brant's gaze narrowed dangerously. "Don't you want to present one of those gifts to your grandson?" he said in a voice that verged on a command.

Doris sighed. For a moment she looked as if she had something else she wanted to say, but then with a motherly shake of her head, she joined her daughter, who was enticing Joey with a large box topped by a blue ribbon.

As his mother joined his sister, Brant moved closer to Jessie. Lowering his voice so that his mother and sister would not overhear, he said, "If you would feel more comfortable in another part of the house, I'll see that you are moved."

He was so close, his breath teased her skin and his light-scented after-shave taunted her senses. She'd feel more comfortable on another continent, she thought, but she said coolly, "The arrangements you've made are fine with me."

Brant nodded and moved toward the mound of boxes, which Joey was busily unwrapping. Perhaps it was unwise to have Joey and Jessie in his wing, he admitted, but what was done was done.

Much later that night, Jessie was tossing restlessly in her bed. She had thought Brant's family must have been a strong factor in his decision to get the divorce. That, of course, made him less independent, less mature, but it also made her feel that their marriage was perhaps more than a mere whim to him. However, that wasn't the case. His mother and sister were warm and generous people. Now that Jessie had met them, she had no doubt they would have accepted her as Brant's wife.

"The truth is that he never loved me," she mut-

tered bitterly. His desire to marry her had been based
on mere infatuation, or mere lust. Whichever, it had
faded fast. He was probably getting tired of being
married to her when the accident happened, and he
had used that as an excuse to give his conscience a
way out.

Too tense to sleep, she rose and walked to the
window. A light snow had fallen during the day,
dusting the ground with a carpet of white. Suddenly
she stiffened. It had been very faint, but she was
certain she had heard a cry of pain. Hurrying into
the nursery, she found Joey sleeping peacefully.

It could have been her imagination, she reasoned
as she returned to her own room. But while the sound
had been very faint, it had still sent a chill racing
through her. Unable to put it out of her mind, she
opened her door and stepped out into the hall. A
moan so low she would not have heard it if she had
been in her room reached her ears. It was followed
by a snarl of anguish.

The sounds were coming from Brant's room. Her
stomach knotted. She felt his pain as if it was her
own. How could she allow a man who did not love
her to wield such a strong hold over her? Still, she
could not make herself turn away.

Crossing to the door of his room, she knocked
gently. A low moan was the only response she received. She tried the knob. It was unlocked. Moon-

light streaming in the window gave the room a sil-
very illumination. Brant was thrashing around on the
bed as if fighting off some savage beast.

"Brant?" she said his name firmly but softly as
she approached.

Instantly the thrashing stopped. "Jess?" he
breathed her name caressingly.

"Are you all right? Can I get you something?"
she offered, fighting to keep the catch out of her
voice.

He groaned again and she moved closer to the bed.
With an impatient kick, he freed himself from the
remainder of his covers. Jess had never known him
to wear pajamas, but to her relief he was wearing a
full set tonight.

Unable to determine if he was in actual pain or
simply caught in the throes of a nightmare, she said
his name again in a questioning tone.

"Jess?" Reaching out, his hand closed around her
arm. "Jess," he murmured, a smile spreading across
his face as he felt the contact.

Before she realized what was happening, he had
pulled her down on top of him. Fire raced through
her as her body pressed against his. She knew she
shouldn't be here. She told herself she should be feeling nothing but loathing at his touch. But loathing
was the last thing she was experiencing.

His mouth sought hers. She ordered herself to turn

away, but the feel of his lips gently roaming her face weakened her will. Instead of thwarting his effort, she allowed him to find her mouth. *You've got to fight this,* she told herself as he gently probed with his tongue, sending currents of searing excitement shooting all the way to her toes.

"You smell so good," he murmured groggily, kissing her neck. "And you taste so good," he growled, nipping her earlobe.

She could not believe her total lack of resistance to his touch. As her body trembled with desire, she ordered herself to push away from him.

"And you feel so good," he added huskily as his hands moved possessively along the curves of her body.

Beneath her, Jessie felt the hardness of his male need. Her legs turned to jelly and her body ached for him. *This is crazy!* she screamed at herself. He had no real feelings for her. She wasn't going to let him use her again just to satisfy his base desire. She had her pride. "Brant, let go," she ordered, struggling to free herself from his grasp.

Suddenly his eyes opened. "Jess?" He said her name in disbelief.

"Let go of me," she ordered again.

"Jess!" He sounded shocked to discover her there. Obeying her command, he released her.

Embarrassment caused her to redden from the top

of her head to the tips of her toes as she realized he'd been asleep and was just now waking up. She'd been incorporated into whatever dream he'd been having. He hadn't even known she was really there.

"What are you doing here?" he demanded in a harsh whisper, watching her clumsy escape from his bed.

"I heard you moaning. I thought you were in pain," she replied shakily, checking the fastening on her robe.

"I was having a nightmare," he growled, shifting into a sitting position and raking his hands through his hair as if he was still trying to wake up. Having Jessie come to his home had been much more dangerous than he had imagined.

"Obviously you're fine," she said with a coolness to cover her embarrassment. Forcing her legs to move, she walked rapidly to the door.

Brant caught up with her in the hall. Circling his hand around her arm, he jerked her to an abrupt halt. "There's no reason for you ever to come into my room again." It was an order.

Jessie felt as if she had been slapped. "I didn't mean to invade your privacy," she snapped indignantly. "I thought you might need help."

"I am quite capable of taking care of myself," he assured her dryly, releasing his hold on her arm.

"That suits me just fine," she retorted. Turning

away from him, she stalked to her room. She caught herself just before she slammed the door. She didn't want to wake up Joey or let the rest of the household know of her confrontation with Brant. She closed the wooden barrier with a restrained push. Then, leaning against it she wrapped her arms around herself as a bitter smile played across her mouth. He hadn't even been awake when he'd kissed her and murmured in her ear, arousing her body to desire. Her chin trembled. How could she be so weak! *It will never happen again,* she promised herself.

Outside in the hall, Brant stood rigidly, staring at the closed door of Jessie's room. For a moment he wondered if maybe he was wrong. Maybe— He cut the thought short. He wasn't ready to face the consequences of telling Jessie everything. That would take more courage than he possessed. "It's better this way," he told himself for the millionth time.

The next morning Jessie was determined to act as if nothing had happened between her and Brant the night before. Brant, too, appeared to have decided that it was best forgotten, because he made no mention of the incident, either. She did notice that he was more guarded than usual around her, but that suited her just fine. The more distance between them the better she liked it.

Following breakfast, Brant took Joey on a tour of

the house and grounds. He invited Jessie to go along, but she refused. She was determined to prove to him and to herself that she had no desire for his company.

Left to her own devices, she wandered into the conservatory. Flowers and green plants filled the room with the odors of spring and summer. The floor was stone, and the domed ceiling and three-quarters of the rounded wall were glass. It was like finding a fairy-tale garden in the midst of a winter storm, she thought as she looked from the bright profusion of flowers to the cold winter landscape beyond the glass barrier.

A friendly but unfamiliar male voice broke into her musings. "You must be Jessie."

Startled, Jessie turned abruptly to find herself facing a handsome, brown-haired, brown-eyed man who, she guessed, was perhaps a year or two younger than Brant. Recalling how Brant had looked before the accident, she could see a strong family resemblance in this stranger's face. He was an inch or so taller than Brant, but less muscular. He did, however, have the same charming smile Brant had used to win her when he'd first come to her inn. "Yes, I'm Jessie," she confirmed politely.

"I'm Brant's cousin on his mother's side. Name's Greg Galloway." He held out his hand in greeting as he moved toward her.

"It's a pleasure to meet you, Mr. Galloway," she replied, accepting the handshake.

"Greg," he corrected, his smile warming even more as he continued to hold her hand. "And I must say my cousin has the most marvelous taste in women."

He was flirting with her! Jess balked. She had no interest in being charmed by any of the males in Brant's family. "Thank you," she replied, politely but firmly working her hand free.

Greg colored with mild embarrassment, as if he hadn't realized he'd been holding her hand captive. Then he laughed lightly at himself. "I apologize if I was too forward. I have to admit that I have been quite curious ever since I learned of Brant's marriage. To be honest, I never thought any woman would get him to the altar. He's always been rather independent and preferred a variety..." His embarrassed flush deepened. "Sorry, I'm always running off at the mouth."

Jessie had the most peculiar feeling that he'd meant to say exactly what he had said. Hearing about Brant's interest in other women brought bile to her throat. She hadn't thought of him as a womanizer when she'd married him. But then she'd been wrong about him from the beginning. "Obviously you were right," she replied coolly. "Our marriage was quite short-lived."

"That was most certainly his loss." Greg's expression was deeply sincere as he again captured her hand. This time he carried it to his lips and kissed the back of it.

"What are you doing here?"

Greg reminded Jessie of a child caught with his hand in the cookie jar. He dropped her hand abruptly and jerked around.

Brant was glaring icily at them both. Focusing his gaze on Greg, he said, "Aren't your parents expecting you for the holiday?"

"I'm flying out to California to join them tomorrow. And I want you to know that getting my airplane tickets changed wasn't easy," he replied, his composure returning along with a mischievous gleam in his eyes. "However, as much as my mother desires my presence at her table for these festive family occasions, her curiosity about your former wife was even greater. After your mother called her to brag about her newly discovered grandmotherhood, my mother called me. First I had to listen to a tirade about how I should find a wife and start producing offspring. Then she told me that she had wrangled me an invitation to join your family for Thanksgiving dinner so I could meet the newest members of the clan." He paused to smile brightly at Jessie. "And I must say I find Jessie charming." Then, turning his gaze back toward Brant, he smiled at the little boy at Brant's side. "And this is my new second cousin?"

"This is Joey," Brant confirmed coolly. He had been walking with Joey holding on to this finger, now he lifted his son into his arms.

Jessie watched the possessive gesture. These two men were definitely not friends, she decided.

Her conclusion was confirmed a little while later. Before Greg barely had time to say hello to Joey, Brant had insisted that his cousin join him for a discussion of a business matter in the study. The two men had left, leaving Joey with Jessie. For a short while, she and Joey looked at the flowers, then he announced he had to go potty. She took him upstairs to the bathroom attached to the nursery.

Brant's study was on the same floor. The door was closed when she and Joey passed it on their way to the nursery. But it was slightly ajar a few minutes later when they came out and started back down the hall.

Doris Mallery's admonishing tones carried into the hall. "I cannot believe you sent Greg off to find his own dinner."

"And I can't believe you invited him in the first place," Brant returned curtly. "This was supposed to be a private family dinner."

"He is family," Doris said, justifying her actions. Her voice became apologetic as she added, "Besides,

I didn't have a choice. My sister called and begged me to invite him. You know how nosy she can be. I didn't see what harm it would do.''

''You would have if you'd seen him with Jess in the conservatory,'' Brant growled. ''He was blatantly flirting with her. You know how competitive he's always been with me. He'd say anything, do anything to win her just for spite, and I don't want to see her hurt.''

Jessie had never approved of eavesdropping, but she froze, unable to make herself continue down the hall. After all, this involved her.

''Da?'' Joey questioned quietly, pointing toward the study door.

Jessie nodded. The harsh concern in Brant's voice had caused a lump in her throat. He didn't want to see her hurt *again,* she corrected, determined to keep his attitude toward her in the proper perspective. For Joey's sake most likely, she added. She thought at any moment Joey would expose them by yelling out to his father, but instead he seemed to sense her uneasiness and remained silent.

''It never occurred to me he would go after Jessie,'' Doris was saying worriedly. ''Perhaps you should warn her.''

Brant snorted. ''You want me to warn her of my cousin's insincerity? Considering her opinion of me,

I doubt she'd take me seriously. It might even cause her to give him more credence.''

The hair on the back of Jessie's neck bristled. Did he really think she was such a fool she would fall for a bit of flattery and the Mallery charm again? ''I've already learned a hard lesson about insincerity,'' she said curtly, pushing the study door fully open and striding into the room. ''You—'' she glared at Brant with proud dignity ''—do not need to warn me about that, nor protect me from it.''

Shock registered on Doris's and Brant's faces.

Suddenly realizing what she had done, Jessie flushed with embarrassment. Pride came to her rescue. ''I was not purposely eavesdropping,'' she said defensively. ''I was going down the hall and heard your voices and my name mentioned.''

Doris was the first to recover. ''There's no reason for you to explain yourself,'' she said, regarding Jessie with motherly concern. ''I'm glad you overheard. It saves me the worry of how to approach you about Greg. He's a very pleasant young man but he *is* a womanizer, and for reasons I have never been able to fathom, ever since he was a child he has acted as if he was in competition with Brant.''

Then Greg has bitten off a great deal more than most men could chew, Jessie thought, her gaze traveling to the silent man watching her with guarded eyes. Her instincts told her that Greg had lied about

Brant's being a womanizer. But that made no real difference. Whether Brant wanted one or a hundred women didn't matter. He didn't want her. She returned her attention to Doris. "Neither of you needs to concern yourself with my well-being," she said. Her gaze swung back to Brant as she added coolly, "I'm perfectly capable of taking care of myself, especially where men are concerned. I learn my lessons well." Suddenly realizing that she had again practically openly admitted how much he had hurt her, she whirled and marched out of the room, firmly closing the door behind her.

"Well that should set your mind at ease about Greg," Doris said to her son.

But Brant didn't look convinced. "He can be very persistent," he said, frowning at the closed door as if Jessie was still there. "And he has a boyish charm that can eventually win over nearly any woman."

Doris gave a heavy sigh. "I'm sorry he had to show up today. But he would've met Jessie sooner or later."

"I know." Brant raked an agitated hand through his hair.

Doris studied him worriedly. "You lied to me. You're still in love with her."

"I just don't want to see her hurt," he growled.

She walked over to him and cupped his face in

her hands. "Maybe you should tell her the truth. Let her make her own decision."

Jerking away from his mother's touch, Brant smiled cynically. Vividly he recalled the look of horror on her face when she'd first seen his burn-scarred chest and back. "You can't even stand to see me without a shirt on. If my own mother finds me that repulsive, I can't expect Jess not to." His shoulders straightened with pride. "I don't want to see that look on her face. It's over between us and it's better left that way."

"I do not find you repulsive," Doris replied defensively. "It's just that when I see those scars, it reminds me of all the pain you went through."

Challenge flashed in Brant's eyes. "Would you like me to remove my shirt to prove my point?"

Doris paled as he began to work the buttons loose. "No," she said around the lump in her throat. Putting her arms around her son, she held him close. "I do love you," she said as a tear trickled down her cheek. "I hope you know that."

"I do," he replied, holding her reassuringly. And he did know his mother loved him. But he also knew how difficult it was for her to look at him. The thought of seeing that same look in Jessie's eyes caused the muscles of his stomach to knot. That was something he couldn't face. *I'm handling this situation the way it has to be handled,* he told himself with grim self-assurance. *There is no future for Jessie and me.*

Immediately upon leaving Brant and his mother in Brant's study, Jessie had gone downstairs and found her way to the recreation room. After Joey had opened his gifts the day before, the majority of them had been moved here. It was a large room at the back of the house with a wide-screen television at one end and a full-sized pool table at the other. A portion of the room had been set aside for Joey. It was furnished with child-size table and chairs. Bookshelves covered two walls of the room, and the shelves in Joey's section were stocked full of brand-new children's books. Brant's family was trying very hard to make her and Joey feel comfortable here, she admitted as she showed Joey how to work one of his toys, but she could never feel truly comfortable in Brant's home. She cringed as she recalled how close she had come to admitting in front of him and his mother how much he had hurt her.

Reaching over, she brushed a lock of hair back from Joey's forehead. "You belong here, but I never will," she said with quiet finality.

"Mind if I join you?" a female voice asked from the doorway.

Glancing over her shoulder, Jessie saw Carol entering. "We'd love to have you join us," she replied, grateful for any interruption that would help her put the scene upstairs out of her mind.

"Guess you met Greg," Carol said, sitting down cross-legged on the rug beside Joey. Her tone was casual, but Jessie heard an anxious note behind it.

It seemed that everyone was concerned about her being susceptible to Greg's charms, she mused wryly. "I met him," she admitted.

For a moment Carol looked hesitant, then her chin lifted determinedly. "I hope you won't think I'm minding your business, but I want to warn you. Greg isn't anything like Brant. You can't trust him. He'll say or do anything to get what he wants."

The two men sounded a lot alike to her, Jessie thought. Aloud she said, "I'll consider your warning."

Carol frowned. "I know what you're thinking. But you mustn't judge Brant too harshly. I know he loved you when he married you." Her expression became suddenly guarded. "The accident changed him."

"If he had really loved me, he couldn't have fallen out of love so quickly," Jessie replied, fighting to keep her voice light, as if what she was saying meant little to her now. "His accident might have changed the outer man, but I doubt it changed the inner one very much."

"If I were in your place, I guess I'd feel the same way," Carol admitted. Her voice took on a pleading note. "But please don't judge my brother too harshly, and don't be fooled by Greg's charm."

"I don't plan to let any man fool me again," Jessie assured her.

Carol looked as if she wanted to make another plea for Brant's sake, but instead, she leaned forward and gave Jessie a hug. "I'm so glad you and Joey are here. I hope you'll come often."

Jessie wasn't ready to make any promises about returning often. But she could not deny the sincerity in Carol's voice. "We'll come again," she said carefully, adding, "You must come up to Maine and visit us."

Straightening, Carol smiled brightly. "I'd love to."

Outwardly Jessie maintained a smile, but inwardly she frowned. Pushing Brant out of her life at the end of the agreed-upon six months was beginning to look impossible. And seeing the way Joey smiled up at Carol, she admitted that discovering Brant's family was good for her son. It was obvious they cared for him, and he seemed to have a natural affinity for them.

For a brief second she found herself thinking how wonderful it would have been to be a part of this family—as Brant's beloved wife. Angrily she berated herself for this moment of fantasy. She was here be-

cause she was Joey's mother. That was the only reason Brant had even considered bringing her back into
his life. Well, he could have his life. She had hers
and it suited her just fine.

Chapter Eight

The first dozen roses arrived around nine o'clock Monday morning. They were long-stemmed, pink blossoms. The attached note read:

> I have never seen a woman look as beautiful as you looked in that room surrounded by flowers.
> Your ardent admirer,
> Greg

The second dozen, deep red ones this time, arrived at nine-thirty. The card read:

> I couldn't resist again placing you in a roomful of blossoms. Your very ardent admirer,
> Greg

"My, My," Haddie said, coming out to find Jessie at the reception desk. "Melody told me you were receiving flowers. Had to come take a look for myself."

Howard, who had come in with Haddie, smiled. "You and Brant settle some of your differences?" he asked.

"Mr. Mallery and I have no differences to settle," Jessie replied.

Haddie gave a huff of indignation as she turned toward Howard. "I told you she was too smart to fall for your boss's line again."

So Howard thought Brant might still be interested in her, Jessie mused. Well, Mr. Green might be an excellent bodyguard, but he was no detective.

Howard met Haddie's gaze with calm command. "Brant isn't the villain you two think he is."

Jessie refused to allow herself to be considered vindictive. "Mr. Mallery and I had a vacation romance. Ours just went a little further than most. We got married and there was a child. But it's over, and we, as two reasonable adults, are working to develop a relationship that will benefit our child."

"Well, I don't know what *reasonable* man would give up as good, kind and sweet a woman as Jessie," Haddie commented pointedly, her gaze still on Howard.

"That part I don't understand myself," Howard

confessed, and was rewarded by a self-righteous smile and nod of agreement from Haddie.

Jessie hated being seen as a victim even more than she disliked being viewed as vindictive. "Don't you two have things to do?" she said with a tone of dismissal.

"I do have a kitchen that needs attending," Haddie replied, not offended by Jessie's curtness. The softness in her eyes said she knew the subject of Brant Mallery's desertion was still painful to the younger woman. Her gaze swung to Howard. "And you said you'd help me clean out those top cupboards."

Howard nodded, but as he turned to follow Haddie, he suddenly glanced back toward Jessie. "You never mentioned who the flowers were from," he said in a casual but coaxing voice.

"They're from Greg Galloway," she replied.

Disapproval shone on Howard's face. "Greg Galloway?"

Haddie had stopped and turned back to face Jessie. "Now why does that name sound familiar?" she mused, frowning in concentration.

"He's not the kind of man you want to get mixed up with," Howard advised in fatherly tones, giving Jessie his full attention.

"So I've already been told by Brant, his mother

and his sister,'' she replied, her tone indicating that these warnings were getting on her nerves.

Howard refused to be put off. "You should heed their advice."

"Will someone please tell me who this Greg Galloway is?" Haddie demanded, her hands on her hips and her gaze swinging from Howard to Jessie and back to Howard.

"He's Brant's cousin," Jessie answered.

"Well, if he's got any Mallery blood in him, I'd suggest you stay away from him," Haddie snapped.

"I have no intention of—" Jessie started to assure her.

"Now I remember why that name sounds so familiar," Haddie interrupted with a dark scowl. "He called and made reservations. He's arriving this afternoon."

"He's nothing but trouble," Howard muttered.

Just what I don't need, Jessie thought acidly. "You two go take care of your chores," she said firmly. "I can handle this on my own."

At that moment the front door opened and the delivery boy from the florist entered with another huge bouquet of roses. This time they were white.

Howard looked dubious, but he said no more. Instead he followed Haddie back toward the kitchen.

Seven bouquets later, Greg arrived.

"I want you to stop the flowers," Jessie ordered him the moment he walked through the door.

His face screwed up into a look of abject pain. "Don't tell me you're one of those women who thinks a single rose is romantic and more than that is garish."

"What I think is that this multitude of bouquets is ridiculous, and that you're wasting your time and money coming up here," she replied.

"Don't let the tourist bureau hear you saying that," he cautioned good-naturedly. "They spend a lot of money trying to coax people to come to Maine."

Refusing to let him charm her, Jessie continued to regard him coolly. "I thought you were supposed to fly out to California."

"I did. But you haunted my dreams—"

Jessie interrupted him. "I'm not interested in your dreams, Mr. Galloway. You're welcome to stay, but don't expect me to give you any of my time."

"Now is that any way for a cousin-in-law to behave?" he chided. "People will think I have the plague."

"*Ex*-cousin-in-law," she corrected.

Shrugging off her correction, he made a boyishly put-upon face. "I suppose Brant warned you about my reputation with women."

"Brant, his mother and his sister," she confirmed.

He gave her a mischievous smile. "It's only because I've never met the *right* woman."

Jessie had seen a great many Casanovas in action,
but Greg Galloway was far and beyond the best.
"That's an extremely old line," she pointed out, admitting to herself that his delivery had made it seem
fresh.

"Brant told me you were an old-fashioned girl. It
seemed like the right thing to say," he said in his
own defense, a crooked smile playing at the corners
of his mouth.

Old-fashioned girl! So that was how Brant cate-
gorized her. Old-fashioned and boring, she added.
Well, maybe she was. She wouldn't apologize for it.
"I'm really very busy," she said curtly. Reaching
behind her, she lifted a key off a hook. "You're in
room seven. Up the stairs and to your left."

"I didn't mean that as an insult," he apologized
quickly. "The fact is, I find it refreshing."

"I really don't care how you find it," she told him
honestly. Although she wasn't willing to admit to
taking Brant's advice on any subject, the fact that his
mother, sister and Howard Green had all confirmed
Brant's opinion of his cousin made her certain she
wanted nothing to do with the man.

"All right, you win," he surrendered good-
humoredly. "But how about letting me take you and
Joey out to dinner? I never even got a chance to

really meet the newest member of our family, and my mother was furious.'' Reading the rejection in her eyes, he held up his hands in a gesture of peace. "I promise not to flirt. I'll think of you purely as family."

Jessie's reply was interrupted by the arrival of another bouquet of flowers. "This has got to stop," she ordered Greg.

"As soon as you say you'll have dinner with me," he bargained. "I'll even agree to leave tomorrow if you ask me to after the meal. I just want a chance to prove I can be a likable fellow."

"You'll leave tomorrow if I ask you to?" Male Mallerys had a decidedly bad effect on her nerves, and the quicker this one left the better.

"Promise," he agreed.

"All right. But we'll dine here in the dining room. At seven," she stipulated.

Giving her a winning smile, Greg picked up his suitcase and, tossing his key in the air and catching it, walked toward the stairs.

The men in Brant's family seemed to have a knack for striking bargains, Jessie mused sourly.

When she went into the kitchen to inform Haddie that she and Joey would be dining with Greg that evening, she saw the worried look that passed between her cook and Howard Green. Obviously, on the point of Brant's cousin, Howard had won Haddie's agreement.

"It's my opinion you shouldn't give that man the time of day," Haddie advised with a disapproving frown.

"He *is* family—Joey's family, anyway," Jessie pointed out. "Our paths are bound to cross every once in a while. It's ridiculous for me to avoid him. Besides, he's promised to leave tomorrow if I ask him to."

"You are planning to ask him to, aren't you?" Haddie demanded worriedly.

Jessie shrugged. It irritated her that everyone seemed to think she needed constant protection from men. She was a mature, sensible adult. She'd made one mistake and she'd learned from it. "I don't see any reason for me to act as if I'm afraid of the man," she replied noncommittally over her shoulder as she left the kitchen.

As she walked back toward the front desk, it dawned on her that it really didn't matter if Greg stayed or left. She was in no danger of falling for him. The only man who had ever held any interest for her was Brant Mallery. Idiot! she cursed herself. The sounds of Joey waking from his nap came through the portable intercom. Pushing Brant out of her mind, she hurried upstairs.

* * *

She had anticipated dinner being a strained affair. But Greg kept his word. He made no passes or flirtatious remarks. He asked about her family and about how she liked running an inn. But there was nothing intrusive about his manner.

Jessie did notice that Joey watched him dubiously.

"I usually get along well with kids," Greg said after trying to coax a smile out of the child and failing. "Guess he's got a lot of his father in him."

Watching her son, Jessie had to admit that not only did he have Brant's coloring, he also had some of Brant's mannerisms. Some Joey had always had, such as the way his mouth formed an almost straight line when he was determined to have his way. Then there were others, such as the way he walked with a firm and forceful stride. He'd picked up that habit since being with his father, who still managed to walk that way despite his limp. "I suppose he does," she admitted.

"Too bad," Greg said sympathetically.

The hair on the back of Jessie's neck bristled. Coming to her son's defense was natural; but the urge to defend Brant, as well, shocked her. "I am extremely pleased with my son, and Brant has proved to be an excellent father," she heard herself saying.

Reaching across the table, Greg took her hand. "I didn't mean to offend you," he apologized. "I know this situation must be hard on you."

"Greg, you and I need to have a private talk," a male voice growled from behind Greg. "You don't mind if we use your office, do you, Jess?"

Looking up in surprise, Jessie saw Brant, his hand coming to rest forcefully on Greg's shoulder. "What are you doing here?" she demanded, keeping her voice low, as she tried not to attract the attention of other diners.

"What *he's* doing here is the question," Brant replied. His hand moved to grasp Greg's upper arm. "Come along, cousin, we need to talk."

"Sorry to eat and run," Greg said with a mischievous grin, allowing Brant to guide him up from the table and out of the dining room.

Jessie flushed with embarrassment as the other diners cast covert glances at her and the two men who were quickly exiting the room. Brant had no right to keep interfering in her life this way!

"Da?" Joey said hopefully, stretching his arms in the direction of the doorway through which Brant's back was disappearing.

"Yes, Da," Jessie replied, lifting Joey out of his chair and carrying him as she walked swiftly after the men. Greg was a guest at her inn, and Brant had no right to come in here and harass him.

The office door was closed when she reached it. Opening it, she stood frozen on the threshold.

Brant's back was toward her and he was so intent

on what he was saying to his cousin that he hadn't heard the door open. "I thought I made it clear I wanted you to stay away from my wife and son," he was saying in a low growl.

His wife. The way he said those words sent a rush of heat racing through Jessie. He sounded like a man fighting for what was his.

"Your *ex*-wife," Greg corrected.

Greg was facing her and Jessie saw the malicious gleam in his eyes. He enjoyed baiting Brant. Seeing her, his expression suddenly became one of boyish innocence.

"Ex-wife," Brant conceded in the same low growl. "I still want you to stay away from her."

"Maybe we should let Jessie decide," Greg suggested, nodding in her direction.

Brant swung around. His jaw tensed. Jess was watching him with a questioning look. Had he exposed himself so openly? His arms ached to hold her. But she wouldn't want to be held by him once she saw what she'd have to look at for the rest of her life, he reminded himself. His expression became shuttered.

"Do you want me to stay or go away?" Greg asked her, exuding his boyish charm.

"Go away," she replied without reservation, her gaze never leaving Brant's face. "And close the door on your way out."

"You heard her, get out!" Brant ordered.

With the look of one who knows when to retreat, Greg gave a shrug and left.

"Da," Joey said, reaching out toward Brant and breaking the heavy silence that had suddenly fallen over the room.

Smiling, Brant took the boy. But Jessie noted the smile didn't reach his eyes. Instead, his expression remained guarded. Her throat was painfully constricted, but she forced herself to speak. "You sounded as if you still thought of me as your wife."

Her betraying eyes had softened to a doelike brown as she watched and waited for his answer. He wanted to take her in his arms and tell her that he would always think of her as his wife. But his rational side reminded him he'd only hurt himself and her more. "I apologize if I sounded possessive," he said gruffly. "My cousin brings out the worst in me."

Possessive! Hot tears burned at the back of her eyes. *Stupid fool!* she berated herself. *You'd hoped it was more. He doesn't love you. He never did.* "I am not your possession," she said tightly. "I will decide who I will see and when I will see them." Afraid she might say something she would regret, she started toward the door.

Suddenly worried he was throwing her into his cousin's arms, Brant blocked her exit. "Look, I know I've probably handled this all wrong,'' he said. ''But you deserve someone better than Greg.''

She glared up at him. ''I don't need you to protect me from dilettante males.''

Brant told himself to keep his mouth shut, but the vision of Greg with Jess was too strong in his mind. ''He was holding your hand.''

For a second she wanted to believe he was jealous, but she knew that was untrue. He had just admitted that his motive was merely possessiveness. *Don't try to fool yourself into thinking it's anything more,* she ordered herself. Her back straightened. ''But I wasn't holding his,'' she snapped. ''Now stay out of my life.'' A thought suddenly struck her. ''Why are you here, anyway?''

''I figured my cousin might try something like this,'' he replied.

''And so you just came up here to check?'' Her eyes flashed as the truth dawned on her. She turned and strode out of the office and into the kitchen. As she suspected, Howard was there helping Haddie. He seemed to spend a great deal of time hanging around her cook, probably so he could pump her for information, Jessie thought. Coming to a halt in front of him, she glared up at him. ''You've been spying on me. I warned you. I want you to pack your things and leave my inn!''

''Jess, you're overreacting,'' Brant said, entering

the kitchen behind her. "Howard is here to protect you and Joey." He was carrying Joey and he paused to run a gentle hand through the boy's hair. "I'm not going to allow you to go unprotected."

"That is not your decision!" she snapped.

"Brant's showing up here isn't entirely Howard's fault," Haddie interjected.

Surprised to hear her cook come to the man's defense, Jessie swung her attention to the older woman. "He called him. I know it."

Haddie nodded. "Yes, he called him," she confirmed. Guilt spread over her face. "But I told him to."

Jessie stared at her in disbelief. "You did what?"

"I told him to," Haddie repeated. "He told me about that Galloway man. I didn't want to see you getting mixed up with the likes of him."

Jessie's gaze swung around the entire assemblage. "Just because I made a mistake three years ago," she growled, her gaze going from Brant, then to her cook and to Howard, "doesn't mean my brain is permanently addled. I learned my lesson. No smooth-talking womanizer is going to turn my head. I am perfectly capable of determining for myself whom I should see and when I want to see them. I would thank all of you if you minded your own business!"

"Mommy," Joey called out to her, an edge of panic in his voice.

As he reached toward her, she took him. "It's all right," she assured him. "I just lost my temper." She gave him a light kiss on the nose. "Busybodies always get to me." Tossing the trio one final hostile glance, she headed toward the door.

"Busybodies?" Joey asked, glancing over her shoulder.

"People who think they know how to run someone else's life better than the person does herself," she elaborated dryly. Leaving the kitchen, she carried Joey up to his room.

She was getting him ready for his bath when Haddie came in. "I've only got a minute," the cook said hurriedly. "I had to leave Howard watching the stove. I just wanted to apologize. I only did what I did because I love you like a daughter and I was worried. I know having Brant Mallery suddenly come into your life again has been difficult."

"It's all right." Putting Joey in his crib for a moment, Jessie gave Haddie a hug. "I shouldn't have lost my temper like that. But I felt as if you were all treating me like a child."

"About Howard…" Haddie said as Jessie released her and attended again to Joey. "Since my Jed died, I'd sort of forgotten how handy it is to have a man around."

"I've noticed that the two of you spend a lot of time together," Jessie replied, studying her cook with interest. She'd also noticed a new spark in Haddie's eyes. She just hadn't realized until now why it was there.

"At first I was making sure he behaved himself." Haddie smiled self-consciously. "But now I've gotten used to having him here."

Jessie shrugged. "He can stay. If I sent him away, Brant would only insist on someone else taking his place."

Relief spread over Haddie's face. "I'd best be getting back to my kitchen before everything burns," she said and hurried away.

"I hope she has better luck with love than I had," Jessie muttered as she picked Joey up and carried him into the bathroom.

Later, after his bath, when she brought him back into his room, she found Brant waiting for them.

"First, I want to apologize to you," he said formally. "You're right. I have no right to go butting into your life the way I have."

"As long as you understand I'm not one of your possessions," she stipulated tightly, "I accept your apology."

"I understand," he replied. It bothered him to let her think he thought of her as a possession. He never had. He'd seen her as a partner, a friend, a lover, someone to share his life with. But that was impossible now. *You can't dwell on what might have been,* he ordered himself. Shifting his gaze away from her, he turned his attention to his son. "I was hoping to make amends with Joey, as well."

"As soon as I get him dressed, you can read him his bedtime story," she said. "You'd like for Daddy to read to you, wouldn't you, Joey?" she coaxed her son.

"Daddy," he said with a smile, his earlier fear forgotten.

"I appreciate your being so understanding," Brant said, watching her.

Jessie glanced at him defiantly. "I would never use our son as a weapon against you."

Reaching out, he traced the line of her jaw with his fingertips. "There was a time when I always knew the right thing to say to you. Now every time I open my mouth, I'm saying the wrong thing."

Despite her determination not to react, his touch left a trail of fire. But even more threatening was the look in his eyes. For a moment there was a wistfulness in those dark brown depths that took Jessie's breath away. Then it was gone. It was just a bit of the Mallery charm, she told herself. It didn't mean anything. As proof, she noted the way he abruptly stopped touching her, as if he suddenly found the contact distasteful. Quickly he turned his full attention to Joey.

Don't ever do that again, Brant ordered himself,

avoiding her gaze and concentrating on his son. The feel of her skin had sent a current of heat rushing up his arm, and again he'd ached to hold her. The urge had been so strong, he'd almost given in. Then he'd pictured the look of horror and rejection he would see in her eyes when she discovered the extent of his injuries. He'd survived a great deal of pain in these past three years, but he couldn't handle that.

To Jessie's chagrin, the heat of his touch continued to linger. How could he still affect her this way? Needing to escape she said, ''I'd better go see if Haddie wants some help in the kitchen.'' Before he could respond, she left the room.

Alone with his son, Brant stared at the closed door. He wanted to go after her. ''But that would only be asking for trouble,'' he informed the child.

Joey gave him a puzzled frown. Then a determined look came into his eyes. ''Book,'' he said, pointing toward the shelf by the wall.

''Book,'' Brant agreed, setting him down so he could make his choice. At least he had their son, whom he could love openly and without reservation. It was a bittersweet consolation.

Downstairs, Jessie discovered Greg on his way out the door, suitcase in hand.

''Howard found me a place to stay a little way down the road,'' he said with an impish grin. ''Thought I'd better make a tactful retreat. When my cousin gets that angry, it's safer to stay out of his way."

"It would be better if you didn't return here at all." It was an order.

Challenge glistened in Greg's eyes. "Are you really going to let him run your life?"

"No," she replied, regarding him levelly. "But I'm also not interested in being a pawn in one of your childish games."

Putting down his suitcase, he captured her hand, then lifted it to his lips and kissed it. "I would never consider you a pawn. To me you will always be a queen." Releasing her, he picked up his suitcase and left.

"Good riddance," Howard said coming up behind her, as the door closed behind Greg.

"And one to go," Jessie muttered under her breath, glancing up the stairs. In firmer tones she said, "I guess I'd better clean Greg's room for Brant. It's the only one we have available."

She was changing the sheets on the bed when Brant found her.

"Joey's asleep," he said, remaining standing in the doorway.

"Your room will be ready in a minute," she informed him, feeling suddenly ill at ease as she remembered the last time they had been in a bedroom together.

His expression remained shuttered as he watched her. "I can't stay. I have a helicopter waiting for me in the church parking lot. It was the closest area we could find to land."

He looked tired, really tired. She told herself not to care, but she did. "You look exhausted. You need to get some rest," she said stiffly.

"I appreciate your concern," he replied in quiet, almost absent, tones. For one brief instant he pictured her lying in his arms. Even after all these years he could still remember how warm and soft she had felt beside him. *Stop it,* he ordered himself.

Jessie saw the sudden haunted look that clouded his eyes and it tore at her heart. Then it was gone and she wondered if she had imagined it. "Joey would worry if you overworked yourself and got sick," she heard herself saying.

He smiled wryly. "I wouldn't want to worry Joey."

Jessie stiffened. She had her pride. How could she still care so much when he cared so little? Anger came to her defense. "If you would spend your time taking care of your business and leaving mine alone, you wouldn't have to lose any sleep."

If she knew how much sleep he'd lost over her, he mused, she'd be shocked. "You're right," he said. "From now on, I'll try to mind my own business." He turned to walk away, then paused and looked back. "Thanks for letting Howard stay."

Jessie shrugged. "I figured if I made him leave, you'd just send someone else."

"I would have," he admitted. His gaze traveled over her. Even in anger she looked inviting. The strain of keeping his distance was wearing down his control. It occurred to him that maybe he should stay away a few days longer than he'd planned. But even as the words formed in his mind, he heard himself saying, "See you this weekend."

Jessie sank onto the bed as she listened to his retreating footsteps. She had been putting a case on a pillow when he'd entered. Now she clutched the pillow to her. She'd never thought she could be so angry at a person and yet care so much about them at the same time.

A bitter smile curled her lips as she remembered the day she had driven into Boston to inform him of his son's existence and discovered he and John Adams were one and the same. After that, she'd been certain the only feeling she could ever have for him again was contempt. She shook her head at her own folly. She cared so much it hurt. "Love," she muttered acidly. "It's supposed to be so wonderful. But in my case, it's a curse."

Chapter Nine

"Jessie, you're a sight for sore eyes."

Jessie glanced up from the papers on her desk at the sound of the familiar voice.

"Guess you're surprised to see me," Ken Darcy said, continuing into her office and closing the door behind him. Jessie's age, he had thick brown hair, striking blue eyes, boyishly handsome features and a smile that caused deep dimples in his cheeks. His parents had first come to Oak Lodge on their honeymoon and had returned every year since, bringing their growing family with them. They'd had three children in all, Ken being the oldest. He and Jessie had become close friends during those summer visits. There was one summer when they were both fifteen that they almost ruined their friendship by developing a crush on one another. But it had died a gentle death and their friendship had survived.

When Ken had gotten married, he'd decided to maintain the family tradition and bring his new bride to the inn for their honeymoon. That had been three years ago and they'd come back each year. But their anniversary was in May. "You're a little early this year," she said worriedly. She knew him well enough to know that his cheerfulness was only a facade.

"Barbara and I broke up. She went home to her mother," he said with a shrug. "Thought I'd come up here to lick my wounds with an old friend. You got a room I can have?"

Jessie liked Barbara. She and Ken seemed to be the perfect couple. Getting up from her desk, Jessie went to him and gave him a hug. "Sure, I've got a room for an old friend. And don't worry, all couples have their bad times. You and Barbara will smooth this over."

"Wish I could believe that," he replied, returning her hug.

During the next couple of days Ken hung around Jessie almost constantly talking about old times, mostly their very youthful years. She listened and enjoyed his company. He knew about Brant, and she

was forced to tell him that Brant had come back into
her life. But she made it sound as businesslike as
possible. When he tried to probe further she managed
to turn the conversation back to his marital difficul-
ties. The truth was, she admitted as Friday came and
she began to tense with the thought of Brant's arrival,
it was nice to have someone else's problems to worry
about.

"I thought maybe you'd let me take you out somewhere for dinner tonight," Ken suggested as they
returned to the lodge late Friday afternoon. They had
taken Joey for a walk in the woods, and now he was
riding on Ken's shoulders as they crossed the wide
front lawn. "I don't want to insult Haddie—no one
could be a better cook than her," he added quickly.
"I just thought you might like a change."

Without even realizing what she was doing, Jessie's gaze shifted to the parking lot. Brant's car was
there. Every muscle in her body suddenly seemed to
freeze. She wasn't ready to spend an evening with
him. "That sounds like fun," she said.

"Good." Ken beamed. "You name the place and
I'll make the reservations."

Jessie had just suggested an Italian restaurant in a
nearby town when Brant came out onto the porch.
"Name's Brant Mallery," he said to Ken before Jessie had time to make the introductions. She noticed
that the smile on his face didn't reach his eyes.

"Ken Darcy," Ken replied, lifting Joey off his shoulders and standing him on the porch. Accepting the handshake, he added, "So you're Jessie's ex. Never met a fool before. Can't believe any man would give up Jessie."

Jessie blushed. "We should be getting Joey inside," she said, giving Ken a sharp nudge.

"Yeah," he replied.

But when he reached down to pick up the boy, Brant was there before him.

"How have you been?" Brant said to Joey, scooping him up.

Joey gave him a hug, then began telling with childlike incoherency about the deer tracks they had seen in the woods.

"Guess Joey's too young to recognize a snake. Looks like you and him get along real well," Ken remarked, following Brant inside.

Jessie glanced warningly at him. He was purposely antagonizing Brant and she didn't want any trouble. The two men were about the same size, and she suddenly realized she was worried he might hurt Brant if he egged Brant into a fight.

"As a matter of fact we do," Brant replied, turning to face Ken squarely.

Suddenly Ken smiled. "Good. Then you can babysit him while Jessie and I go out to dinner tonight." Before either Jessie or Brant could say anything, he tilted Jessie's face upward and gave her a quick kiss on the nose. "Now, if you'll excuse me, I'll go make those reservations."

"New boyfriend?" Brant asked, fighting to keep his hostility under control. He kept telling himself he didn't have any rights where Jessie was concerned, but that didn't make seeing her with another man any easier.

"Old friend," Jessie corrected.

"Old married friend," Brant amended dryly. "I noticed a wedding ring on his finger."

"Old married friend," Jessie conceded. She saw his jaw twitch. Again she found herself wanting to think he was jealous.

It took all of Brant's will to make himself smile. "Have a nice dinner," he said. Turning his full attention to Joey, he began taking off the boy's snowsuit and again listening to Joey's chatter about the prints in the snow.

He couldn't have shut her out more fully if he'd walked into another room and closed the door between them, Jessie thought, watching Brant's back. So much for thinking he might actually be jealous. Leaving him to take care of Joey, she went upstairs to shower and change.

Her spirits sank lower as she dried her hair. Determined to raise them, she pulled out her red wool dress and matching red high heels. The dress was knee-length, with a tight-fitting bodice and full, flared skirt. The sleeves were puffed and the neckline lowcut, exposing a discreet amount of cleavage. It wasn't exactly the kind of dress one usually wore when going out with a platonic friend, but it was festive, and tonight she wanted to feel festive.

She was fastening on her pearl necklace when she heard Brant with Joey in Joey's room. After adding the earrings, she gave her makeup a final check, then shifted her attention to her hair. She had swept it up, gathering it into a loose arrangement of curls on top of her head. To frame her face, she left a few curling tendrils hanging loose. Then she heard Brant's laugh, and her teeth closed over the inside of her bottom lip. She'd worn her hair this way for their wedding, with a crown of flowers surrounding the mass of curls. A rush of heat swept over her as she remembered how Brant had taken her hair down one pin at a time, all the while kissing her neck or nibbling on her earlobe. His touch had ignited an impatient passion within her, but he had refused to rush. When her hair was free, he had undressed her with the same slow, exploring touch as if he wanted to savor the moment forever. By the time he had carried her to their bed, her blood had turned to liquid fire, and her body ached for his with a desire that was a physical pain.

Shocked by the train of her thoughts, she shook

herself back to the present. Her face was flushed and her breath was coming in small gasps. Anger suddenly flashed in her eyes. He had cast her aside. How could she let the memory of his touch arouse her like this! Her jaw tightened in defiance. She would not allow it to happen again. Taking a deep breath, she schooled her face into a look of nonchalance before going into Joey's room to give him a goodbye kiss.

"You look very nice tonight," Brant said. It took all of his control to sound so indifferent. She looked beautiful and too damned inviting to be going out to dinner with a married man. He wanted to block her exit, he wanted... He wanted to take her in his arms and claim her as his own.

"Thanks," she replied in a tone that implied his opinion meant nothing to her. But it was a lie. As she finished saying her goodbye to Joey and headed for the door, she wanted Brant to stop her, to tell her he couldn't let her leave.

"You have got to get that man out of your system," she muttered under her breath as she closed Joey's door and started down the hall.

Inside the room, Brant was staring at the closed door as if he could will her to return. But even if she had, what good would it have done? "You and Jess have no future," he growled to himself. "And the sooner you accept that, the better." Still, he was not ready to sit idly by and let her make a mistake.

Watching from the window of Joey's room, he waited until he saw her drive away with Ken, then he went in search of Howard.

Determined not to allow thoughts of Brant to interfere with her evening, Jessie focused her energies on helping Ken. In the three days he'd been at the inn he'd avoided talking about the problem between him and Barbara. While they ate, he continued to bring up old stories about his and Jessie's childhood adventures. Finally, as they sat drinking a last cup of coffee, she said, "I think it's time for you to tell me what has caused this rift between you and your wife."

Ken frowned down into his cup. "The truth is, Barbara wanted to start a family, and I wasn't sure I was ready to be a father."

"What did she say when you told her that?" Jessie coaxed.

"I didn't tell her," he confessed. "Every time I started to, it sounded childish. So, I made all sorts of excuses. Whenever she brought up the subject of parenthood, I'd tell her I thought kids were too expensive and I'd point out all the problems with raising kids today. Then she'd say her biological clock was ticking and she didn't care about the money or the problems. We'd end up in a huge argument."

Jessie studied him with friendly compassion. "Do you love her?"

He smiled sheepishly. "Yeah. I hate being here without her."

"Then I think you should go home to her and talk to her," Jessie said firmly.

He nodded. "I think you're right. I'll make reservations for a plane home as soon as we get back to the inn. Actually, being here with you and Joey has convinced me that I might like fatherhood, after all."

"I'm glad," Jessie replied.

Love seemed to work out for everyone but her, she thought as they drove back to the lodge.

At the door to her room, Ken kissed her lightly on the tip of her nose. "Thanks," he said.

"You're welcome," she replied.

As he started down the hall toward his room, she felt a prickling sensation on the back of her neck. She turned and saw Brant watching from the head of the stairs.

Brant fought the urge to catch up with Ken and tell him to keep his hands off Jessie. Instead, he approached her and asked with schooled casualness, "Did you have a nice evening?"

"Very," she answered coolly, adding, "I hope Joey behaved himself."

He wanted to grab her and shake some sense into

her. Didn't she know it wasn't smart to go out with a married man? "Yes, he did," Brant confirmed, shoving his hands into the pockets of his slacks.

Jessie stood for a long moment studying him. It was obvious he'd been waiting for her to get home. If he had been an overly protective brother or father, she could have handled it. But he wasn't. He was Brant Mallery, a man toward whom she wanted to feel nothing but indifference. But instead, she couldn't keep herself from hoping that this attention he was paying her was because down deep inside he was jealous...down deep inside he honestly cared for her. *Don't be a fool!* she screamed at herself. *You know it's nothing more than possessiveness. Joey is his only real concern. He doesn't want to compete with a stepfather.* She breathed a frustrated sigh. "I insist that you stop hovering over me. I neither need nor want your guardianship."

Brant was trying to concentrate on what she was saying, but it wasn't working. She was wearing her hair the way she had worn it the day they were married. Ever since he'd seen her earlier in the evening, memories of their wedding and their wedding night had been tormenting him. Just the thought of another man holding her was tearing him apart. "Jess." He said her name with soft longing. Against his will, his hands came out of his pockets and he gently cupped her face.

Jessie stood, unable to move, her gaze trapped in the dark, brooding depths of his eyes. She tried to fight the effect he was having on her, but the feel of his large, strong hands radiated a warmth through her that caused her legs to weaken.

"Jess," he murmured again. He ordered himself to release her and walk away, but her lips looked too inviting. Just once more he wanted to taste her mouth. Just once more.

He was going to kiss her. *Turn away!* she ordered herself. *Fight him!* But she couldn't. *Fool!* she screamed at herself. Her breath locked in her lungs as his mouth found hers. It was only a feather-light contact, but she felt it all the way to the tips of her toes.

She tasted so sweet. Brant's hands left her face. He wanted to put his arms around her, crush her to him. He wanted...*something you can't have!* She wouldn't want him. The thought of her rejection sent a cold chill racing through him. Abruptly he straightened and took a step back.

As his gaze became closed, Jessie's whole body trembled. She'd been ready to fall into his arms again! Now he was standing there like an iceberg. *And I'm the* Titanic! A bitter anger filled her. "How could you...!" she stammered in a low growl. "How could I...?" she demanded with even more venom. She was so furious, her breath was coming in gasps.

"Get out of my life and stay out!" she ordered. She couldn't even think coherently she was so enraged, both at him and at her own weakness for him. Unable to face him a moment longer, her hand found the knob of her door, and in one fluid movement she escaped into her room. Locking the wooden barrier, she leaned against it. Hot tears of frustration burned in her eyes.

Brant stood frozen in the hall staring at the space she had occupied only a moment earlier. What had he done? The hurt and anger he'd seen on her face frightened him. He didn't know what she might do. Taking a step forward, he knocked lightly on her door.

She opened it a crack. He was standing there looking down at her worriedly. Cynicism etched itself into her features. The concern on his face wasn't going to fool her. It wasn't for her. He was just worried about her cutting off his access to his son. "Go away," she said, enunciating each word in a cold clipped tone.

"Jess..." he began in a voice filled with apology. But before he could get a second word out, she had closed the door.

Brant raked a hand through his hair. Maybe it would be best to wait until morning. His gaze shifted down the hall. Morning might be too late. He'd never seen Jessie so angry or so hurt, and Ken Darcy was only four doors away. The image of her going to the man for comfort shook him. He couldn't wait until morning. He had to make amends tonight. Reaching into his pocket, he found the key to Joey's room.

Standing with her back pressed against the door, her jaw taut and her eyes clamped shut to hold back the tears she refused to allow to escape, Jessie did not hear him open the door of her son's room. Her mind was too full of its own turmoil. She hated Brant Mallery for his ability to hurt her, and she hated herself for being too weak to fight. If she never saw him again she could die happy.

"Jess, we need to talk."

Her eyes popped open. He was there in her room. It was as if some evil spell hung over her and she couldn't escape from her torment. It was no evil spell, she berated herself. He'd come in through Joey's room and the bathroom. "Get out!" she hissed.

Brant had faced many an angry man, but none of them had been as formidable as the woman in front of him. "Jess, I want to apologize."

She glared at him. She was beyond worrying about being humiliated. Her anger had taken complete control. "Apologize? You want to apologize? For what? For kissing me just now? Another big mistake, right? Or do you want to apologize for marrying me in the first place? Or producing a son so that we can never be fully free of one another?''

Brant studied her uneasily. She hated him. He couldn't blame her. But he had to make her see reason, at least where Ken Darcy was concerned. He couldn't let her throw herself away on a married man. If she did, it would be his fault. ''I came to apologize for interfering in your life,'' he said levelly.

She had been wrong. Her outspokenness had embarrassed her. She'd never wanted him to see the extent of the anguish he could cause her. Scraping together her dignity, she faced him coldly. ''Fine. You've apologized. Now get out.''

''I know you're in no mood to listen to me,'' he said gruffly. ''But I don't want to see you wasting yourself on someone like Ken Darcy. So he had a fight with his wife. Now he's here using you to make himself feel better. But as long as he's still married he might go back to his wife.''

Jessie glared at him. ''In one breath you apologize for interfering with my life, and in the next you have the nerve to warn me about getting involved with Ken?''

''I just don't want to see you get hurt,'' he replied stiffly.

He didn't want to see her get hurt? she fumed. That was the final straw! ''First you decided that

Philip wasn't right for me. Then you were worried
I'd fall for Greg and his smooth charm. Now you
want to warn me about Ken." She told herself to
stop and think before she went any further, but her
anger was too great to be swayed by reason. "You
don't want me, but you're full of advice about anyone I might want. Well, I'm not interested in your
advice."

Brant groaned. He was practically throwing her
into Ken Darcy's arms! In his mind's eye he saw her
rushing to Darcy for solace. The bile rose in his
throat. His control snapped. "Not want you?" he
growled. "Oh, I want you, Jess. At night I lie awake
thinking about having you in my arms. Every time I
look at you, I want to crush you to me and never let
go."

A silence filled the room. Realizing what he had
said, Brant stood frozen, fighting to regain his control.

Jessie stared at him in shocked disbelief. He'd said
he wanted her! But he didn't love her, she reminded
herself harshly. She'd been hurt before because she'd
let herself believe that he honestly cared for her.
"You're talking about lust," she snarled. "And with
you, that's a momentary thing where I'm concerned."

Brant drew a shaky breath. There was no way to
turn back now. He was finished lying. Besides, it

hadn't worked. He'd only made a huge mess of this whole situation and caused Jessie to hate him even more. "I wish it was only lust. That would fade with time. I'd hoped, for both our sakes, my feelings for you would change. But they haven't. I love you, Jess. I've always loved you."

Her hands balled into fists. She ached to believe him. But none of this made any sense. "I don't understand." The pain his rejection had caused etched itself into her face. "If you love me, why have you insisted on keeping this distance between us?" Deep accusation flashed in her eyes. "You don't have any excuse. You can walk. You've got a new face."

He smiled a crooked, bittersweet smile. "What you can see isn't so bad," he conceded. He was wearing a knit shirt with his slacks. Reaching down, he caught it by the hem. "But I couldn't ask you to live with this." Raising it, he exposed his chest.

Jessie's jaw trembled at the sight of the massive burn scars. He turned and she followed their path across his back.

Brant heard her gasp of horror and saw the shock on her face. He was living his worst nightmare. Jerking his shirt down, he stalked out of the room. She'd reacted the way he'd expected her to react—the way he had known she would react. He repulsed her!

Jessie stood frozen. Scars! He'd stayed away from her because of a few scars? She suddenly became mobile. Cursing his male pride under her breath, she strode down the hall and knocked on his door.

Brant considered not answering. Her pity was the last thing in this world he wanted.

Forgetting about her guests, she knocked louder.

He'd have to face her sooner or later, he told himself. Steeling himself against her pity, he opened the door. But pity wasn't what waited for him on the other side. It was anger that burned in her eyes.

Brushing past him, she entered his room. When he stepped back to give her space, she kicked the door closed with the heel of her shoe. "You must think I'm an extremely shallow person," she snapped. "First you turn away from me because you don't want to burden me with a husband who might not have a decent-enough face or one who might never walk again." She was trembling with rage but she went on, "I loved you so much I wouldn't have cared what you looked like or if you'd had to spend the rest of your life in a wheelchair—just as long as we were together. Then when those obstacles were overcome, you decided that I wasn't strong enough to deal with a few scars! You know, I really don't understand how you could even claim to love someone you consider so weak-minded."

Brant stood staring at her. She was telling him that he'd made all the wrong decisions, and he wanted to believe her. But he wasn't certain the reality of the situation had fully sunk into her mind. "You'd better think about what you're saying," he cautioned. He knew what he had to do. Still it took every ounce of self-discipline he had to discard his shirt. "Can you honestly face living with this body for a lifetime?"

She saw the anguish on his face, and her anger weakened. Taking a step toward him, she let her fingers travel lightly over the scarring. She felt no revulsion. She was just glad he had survived. The thought of the suffering his injuries had put him through sent a chill through her. She should have been there for him—but he hadn't allowed her that. Her anger again surfaced. "I can live with the scars," she replied, her hand dropping to her side as she took a step back, putting distance between them. "But I'm not certain I want to live with you." A challenge filled her eyes. "If I had been the one in the accident, would you have turned away from me?"

Her question startled him. A protectiveness etched itself deep into his features. "No," he said without reservation.

The years of pent-up rage and pain exploded within her. "You didn't even give me the chance to make that decision," she seethed. "You made it for me. You pushed me out of your life. You left me feeling used and unwanted. You deserted me!"

A cold fear swept over Brant. For a moment, when

she'd touched his scarred chest and not recoiled, he had been filled with a hope that they *could* have a life together. Now it occurred to him that he might have hurt her too much for her to ever care for him again. "I know now I did everything wrong," he said, studying her for any sign of forgiveness. "I was trying to be unselfish. Or maybe I was being very selfish. I couldn't face your rejection." A cynical smile tilted one corner of his mouth. "I've never been so afraid of anything in my life as I was of seeing you looking at me with an expression of revulsion and horror. Or worse, pity."

Jessie stared into the pleading depths of his eyes and knew that he had suffered as much as she had. "You are the most infuriating man I have ever known." Her anger faded as tears began to roll down her cheeks. She had loved him then and she loved him now. "I need you to hold me," she choked out.

Brant bridged the distance between them in one long stride. Wrapping his arms around her, he crushed her to him. "You're going to have to forgive me, Jess," he said into her hair, "because I haven't got the strength to make myself let you go—not ever."

She buried her face in his neck and circled her arms around him. "Don't you ever, ever try."

"I hope this means you'll marry me again," he said, kissing the top of her head.

She tilted her face up to meet his gaze. "If you promise to listen more closely to the vows this time," she stipulated.

"'In sickness and in health, till death do us part,'" he replied solemnly.

Fire glittered in her eyes. "That's exactly right, and don't you ever forget it."

"Never," he promised, his mouth finding hers for a kiss, hungry for the taste of her.

Five days later Jessie awoke beside her new husband. Snuggling against him, she kissed him as happy memories of their wedding the afternoon before played through her mind. For the third time, Jessie had closed the inn. "Third time's the charm," she'd told Brant, and he confirmed that with a kiss that made her knees weaken.

The wedding had been a small, intimate affair. Carol and Doris had flown in for it. Haddie had been Jessie's attendant and Howard had been Brant's best man. Joey had stood happily between his father and Howard, and handed Brant the ring.

The only tense moment of the day was when Philip came by. He wanted to speak to Brant alone, but Jessie insisted on being present.

"Since Jessica has no father, I feel it is my duty as her friend and lawyer to have a few words with you," Philip addressed Brant when the three of them were cloistered in Jessie's office. "I can understand why you acted the way you did. But I don't want to see Jessica hurt again. I want your word that you will never underestimate her again."

"You have my word on that," Brant replied, holding his hand out to put his seal on the promise.

"Then I wish you both the very best," Philip said, accepting the handshake and then giving Jessie a hug.

They'd asked him to stay for the wedding, but he'd refused. He had a luncheon date with a new female attorney who had just arrived in town. She was a tall, redhead with an air of self-assurance that would make her a match for any man. Jessie also noticed that there was a gleam in Philip's eyes that hadn't been there when he'd been dating her. He and his redhead might not have as comfortable a relationship as the two of them had had, Jessie mused with a smile as she waved goodbye to him from the porch, but she guessed it would be a lot more exciting.

Glancing at the clock on the bedside table, Jessie breathed a resigned sigh and started to work her way quietly out of the bed.

The arm around her tightened. "I want your word you'll be back here in two minutes," a gruff male voice demanded.

Jessie turned to see Brant watching her. "I thought you were asleep."

"I've been lying here for the past hour thinking about what a lucky guy I am," he replied. With a crooked smile, as he remembered something Ken Darcy had said, he added, "Not every fool gets a second chance."

"You're right," she agreed mischievously, kissing him quickly. The arm around her tightened, drawing her closer to him. Desire began to spread through her. "I've really got to go check on Joey," she said regretfully.

Brant's hold remained firm. "I checked on him while you were sleeping. He's being spoiled rotten by Haddie, my mother and my sister. I'm the man in your life who needs your attention at the moment."

Laughing softly, Jessie relaxed against him. "You have it," she assured him, trailing kisses along the strong line of his jaw.

"I hope you'll accept this, this time," he said, reaching over to the bedside table and returning with the gift she had refused the day of Joey's birthday.

"This time, I will," she conceded, taking the package from him. Shifting onto her back, she opened it. Inside was an ornate silver box shaped like a treasure chest. "It's beautiful," she said, lifting it out of its packaging.

"The important part of the gift is inside," he informed her.

Opening the chest, she discovered an almost clear,

roughly shaped rock with a circumference about the
size of a nickel.

"It's an uncut diamond," Brant explained as she
lifted it out for a closer look. "My great-grandfather
brought it back with him from one of his many
travels. He was going to have it cut and made into a
ring for my great-grandmother, but she insisted on
keeping it the way it was. She said that in that form
it reminded her of him. He had a tough, sometimes
bullheaded, exterior. But she knew that, inside, his
love for her was as strong and steadfast as the diamond in this stone. She gave it to me because I reminded her of my great-grandfather." Shifting onto
an elbow, he raised himself so he could look down
into Jessie's face. "She was right. I want you to
know, Jess, that my love for you is as lasting as that
stone."

The depth of emotion she saw etched in his face
caused her chin to tremble. "I feel as if I've waited
a lifetime to hear you say that."

Seeing the flash of pain in her eyes, Brant drew
her close. "I can see I have a lot of making up to
do."

Jessie's body ignited beneath his touch. "Now is
as good a time as any to begin," she suggested, replacing the stone in the box and setting the box on

the table.

"Definitely a good time to begin," he agreed huskily.

* * * * *

SPECIAL EDITION

Stories of love and life, these powerful novels are tales that you can identify with— romances with "something special" added in!

Fall in love with the stories of authors such as **Nora Roberts, Diana Palmer, Ginna Gray** and many more of your special favorites—as well as wonderful new voices!

Special Edition brings you entertainment for the heart!

SSE-GEN

SILHOUETTE®
Desire®

Do you want...

Dangerously handsome heroes

Evocative, everlasting love stories

Sizzling and tantalizing sensuality

Incredibly sexy miniseries like **MAN OF THE MONTH**

Red-hot romance

Enticing entertainment that can't be beat!

You'll find all of this, and much *more* each and every month in **SILHOUETTE DESIRE**. Don't miss these unforgettable love stories by some of romance's hottest authors. Silhouette Desire—where your fantasies will always come true....

DES-GEN

INTIMATE MOMENTS®

Silhouette®

If you've got the time...
We've got the
INTIMATE MOMENTS

Passion. Suspense. Desire. Drama. Enter a world that's larger than life, where men and women overcome life's greatest odds for the ultimate prize: love. Nonstop excitement is closer than you think...in Silhouette Intimate Moments!

Silhouette®

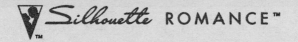

Silhouette ROMANCE™

What's a single dad to do when he needs a wife by next Thursday?

Who's a confirmed bachelor to call when he finds a baby on his doorstep?

How does a plain Jane in love with her gorgeous boss get him to notice her?

From classic love stories to romantic comedies to emotional heart tuggers, **Silhouette Romance** offers six irresistible novels every month by some of your favorite authors! Such as…beloved bestsellers **Diana Palmer, Annette Broadrick, Suzanne Carey, Elizabeth August** and **Marie Ferrarella,** to name just a few—and some sure to become favorites!

Fabulous Fathers…Bundles of Joy…Miniseries…
Months of blushing brides and convenient weddings…
Holiday celebrations… You'll find all this and much more
in **Silhouette Romance**—always emotional, always
enjoyable, always about love!